Cyrus Cole

The Auroraphone

A Romance

Cyrus Cole

The Auroraphone
A Romance

ISBN/EAN: 9783337347765

Printed in Europe, USA, Canada, Australia, Japan

Cover: Foto ©Andreas Hilbeck / pixelio.de

More available books at **www.hansebooks.com**

AURORAPHONE

𝕬 𝕽𝔬𝔪𝔞𝔫𝔠𝔢

BY

CYRUS COLE

———•◆•———

CHICAGO
CHARLES H. KERR & COMPANY
175 DEARBORN STREET
1890

What tonic can be more inspiriting and healthful than an adventure? It gives back to the blood all its youth.—*Emerson*.

PREFACE.

It is perhaps to be regretted that the Auroraphone was not discovered by men of mature years rather than by mere boys, whose inexperience and facetiousness are apt to detract from the dignity, and possibly lead us to undervalue the importance, of its revelations. Youth necessarily imparts to its narrations some of its own buoyancy of spirits, and concerns itself but little with the fitness of things. It was the realization of this that prompted Mr. Karbun to turn his manuscript over to me with the request that I "tone it down and sober it up somewhat." After reading it I could but feel that he was wise in this, and the heaviness of heart that oppresses the conscientious expurgator of another's manuscript seized upon me. Then came the thought that as nature had delegated to boys the discovery of the wonderful instrument it was more fitting that one of their number should write the history in his own way, and instead of expunging I supply this preface.

I trust that the trivial nature of the incidents

attending the discovery of the Auroraphone and its subsequent revelations will in no wise militate against the true import of the latter. While the Creetan philosophy, as presented by the two functionaries of that progressive people, may be barren of literary grace, deficient in details and wanting in perspicuity, yet time may prove that in justice, charity and humanity it leads the world.

CYRUS COLE.

GARDEN CITY, KANSAS,
JULY 14, 1890.

CONTENTS.

BOOK I.

THE VOYAGE OF THE BEDFORD.

BOOK II.

TEN YEARS LATER.

BOOK I

THE VOYAGE OF THE BEDFORD

THE AURORAPHONE.

CHAPTER I.

THE HIGHWAYMEN.

SEE Naples and die! No; it is not the incidents of
a voyage to Naples that I am about to chronicle.
Hectic fevers were responsible for my queer hallucination that the modern prescription, "See the Rocky
Mountains and live," was far more pertinent than the
musty aphorism of the Neapolitan boomers. For a
year, Death, with his usual want of discrimination,
had been hinting that I was a mark too dazzlingly
conspicuous to escape his icy shafts. But I fled to
Colorado's salubrious climate—that region of ozone,
mountain streams and cloudless skies which has repeatedly proved that the much-vaunted connoisseur
in shining marks is an arrant humbug after all.
Many a precocious young man wooed by the dark
angel has found refuge in the Centennial State, where
he lives a life in no wise distinguishable from the common herd, and just as happy and contented as if he
had died young, regretted as an irreparable loss to
the world.

In the summer of 188— I was living at Colorado
Springs, dividing pleasure and profit,—the pleasure of

regaining my health amidst such grand scenes, my own; the profit, landlords' and liverymen's. Going to the post-office one June morning, the postal deity that presided over the window bearing the beautiful legend, "A to K," greeted me with a smile which, had it expanded a bit more, would have meant registered letter; but it stopped at ordinary letter, and he handed me one, the super-scription of which at once carried me back to the old home in Iowa. To my surprise, however, the post-mark read "Las Animas, Colo." It proved to be from my cousin Melvin S., and informed me that he and one of my old school-mates, James B., were en route with wagon and team for the Springs. I was ordered to be in readiness to take passage in the prairie schooner Bedford and accompany them on a trip through the mountains. A week later they made port, and laying in some additional supplies we bore southwest toward Cañon City. Our objective point was Wagon Wheel Gap, a beautiful mountain resort far up toward the head-waters of the Rio Grande.

My kinsman and friend were pedagogues, whom the worry and confinement of teaching had worn down to bundles of shattered nerves, and a summer's "roughing it" was to tone them up and fit them for their preceptorial duties the coming winter. They had driven through from Iowa and were already somewhat improved in health, and decidedly sun-burned and weather-beaten in appearance.

Mr. B., or Jim, as I shall call him, owned the outfit, —a handsome pair of mules, a new wagon with good cover, and all the conveniences for camping out. The tool-box bolted on the front end of the wagon contained a saw, hatchet, nails, brace and bits, monkey-wrench, ball of heavy twine, and many other things, showing that the school-master's tool-box was but an evolution of the school-boy's pocket. A box in the rear end of the wagon was so arranged that the lid turned down, making a table, while in the various compartments of the box were stored our provisions and dishes. Two small boxes, one fastened on each side of the wagon, held our cooking utensils. Thus the interior of our schooner was reserved for an elegant *salon* by day and a luxurious state-room by night.

We differed, perhaps, from any other tourists who have made a wagon journey through the mountains, in that we had no fire-arms. We were not hunters, and contended that any one who attended strictly to his own business had no need of weapons even in the wild West. About a year previous to our trip, a friend in the East had sent me an account against a man living in the Springs, and with consummate shrewdness I had induced the debtor to give me a revolver and two boxes of cartridges for the bad debt, but had subsequently loaned the revolver and one box of the cartridges to a party who never returned them. However, I had one box of the cartridges, which I retained as my fee for collecting the bill, and by mere chance they were now in my valise, which was fraternizing with those of my comrades under the spring seat in the front end of the wagon. In lieu of fire-arms we had a volume of poems, a text-book on English Literature, a Bible, and Spencer's First Principles. We were three young, inexperienced, inoffensive sight-seers, doing the mountains for pleasure and health.

Our first stop was for dinner at the mouth of Dead Man's Cañon, about thirteen miles south of the Springs. A dead man, supposed to have been murdered, had been found in the cañon, and so gave rise to its lugubrious name. Near the scene of the tragedy was an old house which still bore witness to the bloody deed in many uncanny manifestations. It happened that I had been boarding with a Mr. S., who from actual experience could vouch for the fact that the house was infested with ghosts. Mr. S. had done considerable teaming between the Springs and Cañon City, and passed the house every few days. On one trip he and a fellow-teamster had concluded to camp at the haunted house, sleep within its ghostly precincts and see if there was any truth in the rumors afloat concerning its nocturnal visitants from the spiritual world. At the time of retiring they had spread their blankets on the rough floor of the one room, brought in their harnesses, hanging them up on an old gun-rack made of deer's horns, shut and barred the doors and lain down with their clothes on, with no other thought than that they should enjoy uninterrupted repose till morning. They had just fallen into their first sleep when the harnesses were dashed violently to the floor and the doors flew open, and closed with a loud crash. The two men sprang up, but found nothing of the ghost. The doors were found closed and barred just as they had left them. They made a careful search of the premises inside and out, but still the ghost eluded them. They hung up the harnesses, again fastened the doors, and lay down determined they would not be caught napping this time. Half an hour later, while both men were wide awake and keenly alert, the same things occurred. Badly frightened, they quickly harnessed their teams, hitched up and drove on a few miles and camped for the remainder of the night.

To boys whose ages ranged from eighteen to twenty, here was presented the chance of a lifetime. It came out, after I told the story, that we had all been longing to investigate in person a genuinely haunted house. Dinner over, we entered the sepulchral shades of the cañon and drove toward the ghost's habitation, and when we arrived there—journeyed on without delay. Considering the state of our nerves, it was, perhaps, the wisest thing to do.

Two miles further and we emerged from the gloomy cañon into a park of gently rolling prairie, environed by shadowy mountain chains. It was coming out of the dark and narrow home of the dead, where chill and gruesome specters terrify, into the bright and happy better-land. The afternoon was delightful. There was that soft, hazy condition of the atmosphere which tones down the rugged outlines of distant mountains, blending them into pictures of such exquisite beauty and mystic coloring, that we easily imagined we were approaching the Delectable

Mountains. The fancy merged into certainty as luminous masses, "with purple mist obscured," presently resolved themselves into magnificent structures which the *mirage* surrounded with waving foliage and sparkling pools, and we soon fell to speculating as to which of the stately, shimmering mansions, seen vista-like through the engirdling hills, were being prepared for our reception.

For two days we wended our way through these semi-celestial scenes which rather incongruously terminate in the Cañon City oil fields. Driving through Cañon City, we had our choice of crossing the Arkansas on the "condemned" bridge that then spanned the river, or fording it. We preferred the latter, though it seemed risky to drive into the noisy, foaming torrent. The danger was more apparent than real, for while the wild waters played all sorts of pranks, they did no actual harm. Occasionally a frolicsome current would strike our mules and try to sweep their legs from under them, but would dart away with a gurgling titter just in time to escape the lunges they made to recover their equilibrium. Then a more mischievous wave would swing our schooner against a rock, shaking her up from stem to stern, and, rejoicing at our trepidation, rush on with a boisterous laugh, while numerous other eddies and swirls would hurry off to the neighboring rocks fairly frothing over with merriment as they told the joke. Rollicking, singing, and laughing, the happy waters go, a little wild and turbulent now, but soon to settle down into the quiet channels of business life in the irrigated districts of

Western Kansas. As we drove out, the brightened wheels scattered showers of diamonds, which glistened like true brilliants in the last rays of the setting sun. We struck camp for the night near the river.

The following day found us threading the mazes of Oak Creek Cañon, greeted at every turn by new and fantastic formations of gray rock and red sand-stone. That night we camped in the vicinity of Silver Cliff, and the next day and night were spent at this mining camp. Here we were initiated into the mysteries of shafting, blasting, leads, "big finds," "pay dirt," and "grub stakes." The Bull Domingo mine was at that time in possession of an armed force, and another party of men was arming preparatory to contesting the rights of ownership. War and fighting, seasoned with bloody combats and hand-to-hand encounters, were the popular themes, and the stories of thrilling adventures with horse-thieves and road-agents we heard, filled us with admiration for the daring and prowess of the stalwart miners. We learned especially of the frightful depredations that were being committed by a band of horse-thieves who had their rendezvous in the Sangre de Cristo range of mountains which we must cross at Mosco Pass. We were given much good advice and many serious admonitions to be very watchful of our team. With numerous warm hand-shakes and expressions of good will from the big-hearted, friendly miners, we departed on the morning of the memorable 1st of July.

Our stay at Silver Cliff had not on the whole had a tonic effect on our nerves, and we lost many of the

2

beauties of Wet Mountain Valley in our growing fears
of horse-thieves. In our hurry to get beyond the
mountains we did not stop, as usual, for dinner, and
a little after noon, with longing looks backward at
the peaceful, happy valley, we began the ascent of the
pass. An hour's drive brought us to the summit,
and far away, over intervening hills, we could see portions of the San Luis Valley. But we had the descent
yet to make before we should reach the haven of
safety. When about one-third the way down, there
burst upon our view a wonderful scene—a scene impressive and grotesque rather than grand. The
principal feature was a chain of stupendous sand
hills—The Great Sand Dunes, they are called—extending from the foot of the mountains far out into the
valley. These sand hills are different from any others
I have seen in the West. They are composed of fine
glittering sand which curls and glistens like little rip-
pling waves with every breeze. A stronger wind
gathers up multitudes of the gleaming particles into
a luminous cloud, which rolls along catching the sunlight, now and then flashing out golden and purple
tints, the gorgeousness of which fairly dazzles the beholder. The moving shadows that play in the deep
valleys and around the sharp peaks, as the cloud is
carried across the hills, heighten the effect into something altogether novel and enchanting. Then the
wind lulls, the cloud settles, and the huge, uncouth
peaks throw monster shadows on the yellow sand,
weird and startling in the extreme. Changing their
forms at the caprice of the winds, these hills never

present the same appearance for any length of time, but constantly wreathe and twine themselves into ever-varying and unique shapes.

While we greatly enjoyed these quaint scenes, there had nevertheless come over us a feeling of depression, which on comparing notes developed into a well defined presentiment of impending danger. However, we made the descent without serious interruption. Near the foot of the mountain we came to a toll-gate, the keeper of which was anything but prepossessing in appearance. In answer to our inquiries about the route, he informed us that it was sixty miles to Del Norte, that the stream a quarter of a mile further on was the only water for many miles, and that the country was a sandy sage-brush plain through which we would have much difficulty in keeping the road. Paying the toll fee we drove on to the stream, a broad shallow river, but did not cross, as the road turned and ran parallel with it as far as we could see. The water, however, all sank into the sand a little way below us. As we were compelled to camp in this vicinity, the level, grassy plain in which we found ourselves seemed providential. Driving up the stream fifty yards we turned the wagon facing the river and camped for the night, though the sun was yet an hour high.

Just as we got our mules tethered, a party of four men with wagon and team drove down to the stream, watered their horses, talked awhile in low tones and then drove down the road fifty yards and camped.

The new-comers wore broad-brimmed white hats,

blue flannel shirts, corduroy trowsers, and top boots. They were dirt-begrimed and weather-beaten, and altogether a hard looking lot. They drove a splendid pair of bays, much finer horseflesh, indeed, than men of their ilk would come by honestly. Their camping there we surmised was all a sham — part of a well laid plan to get Jim's mules. They would probably rob us of our few personal effects, and no doubt their motto was that dead men tell no tales. We thought seriously of pushing on immediately at the risk of getting lost and perishing miserably in the desert. But even if we resumed our journey we could not escape them, nor would it help the matter any to turn back; indeed, it would better suit their purpose to catch us in the deep solitudes of the desert or the lonely wilds of the mountain pass.

Our neighbors were soon busy making preparations for supper, and there was nothing for us to do but to follow their example. Among our stores were some canned pears and cherries which we thought were extremely fine, and much on the same principle that the boy says to the big dog he fears is going to eat him up, "Poor doggie," we now concluded to take two cans of the fruit and offer it to our fellow-campers. Intent on this gastronomic peace-mission we all started over, but to our mortification and alarm the four men quickly laid down their cooking implements and deliberately picked up two Winchester rifles, and as many Smith & Wesson revolvers, which we had not before seen, and sauntered off down toward the stream. In the face of such a rebuff we could but return, burdened with greater apprehensions than ever. While we had suspected that they were armed, yet this abrupt discovery of the fact was anything but pleasant.

We now deeply regretted that we had not provided ourselves with arms. It was even mentioned as an unaccountable oversight that we had not procured a small cannon, or, for that matter, a large one would not have come amiss. But unfortunately we had not, and if anything was to be done it must be through strategy. I had been thinking about my cartridges and I now suggested that we devise some means of firing off a few of them, and so make the enemy think we were also armed. We fixed upon a plan and immediately set about to put it into execution.

The wagons stood parallel with each other about one hundred yards apart. By working on the far side of our wagon our movements would be practically hidden from the horse-thieves. From our California brake we took the rubbers, two pieces of hard wood, ten inches long, four wide and two thick, and with the brace and bit of the proper size bored three holes through one of the pieces. These three holes, about one-half inch apart, held the cartridges, which were center fire. Through the other piece of wood were bored three small holes so as to strike the centers of the first three holes when the two rubbers were properly adjusted. Putting in three cartridges the rubbers were bound tightly together with baling wire, a sharp pointed nail was inserted in one of the small holes to receive the blow from the hatchet, and our battery of three pieces was completed. It was then bound securely to the rear wheel and standard of the wagon with baling wire. We next fixed up a target. Two sticks, one five, the other three feet in length, and both about two inches in diameter, and the ball of twine, furnished the material. The shorter stick with the twine tied to the lower end of it was the trigger or brace to support the other stick, the target proper. Mel took the two sticks, and letting the ends drag in the grass so as to conceal the string, went out about one hundred yards to the rear of the wagon. I was lying down in the grass and paid out the twine. Mel leaned the target against the brace, then came back and took a position as if to shoot, nothing but his legs being visible to those on the opposite side of our wagon. Jim, hatchet in hand, acted as gunner. The critical moment had arrived.

Ready.

The gunner hit the nail.

Bang!

I had jerked the string as Jim made the stroke and the target went down beautifully. Everything worked to a charm.

I now went out and set up the target. Mel, in the meantime, had lain down near the string. I took the marksman's position this time. Again the battery spoke, and the target went down as before. I then relieved the gunner and he was the next marksman, proving himself as good a shot as either of us.

The target was then taken out much farther, the battery reloaded and the performance repeated, the target going down with a certainty that must have astonished the enemy, who, we were glad to see, had become very interested spectators. Even once when the gunner missed the nail the target fell with the same deadly accuracy. Of course the enemy would think it had fallen accidentally. But after all they might think that we had but one revolver—so far we had been shooting with the monkey-wrench. To undeceive them, in case they did labor under such hallucination, we concluded to shoot off three cartridges at once, which we could easily do by putting in three nails, and hitting them with the flat of the hatchet. To add to the effect we were each to have a weapon. Mel had the monkey-wrench, Jim took the wagon hammer, which in times of peace served to hold the double-tree on the wagon tongue; I took a half-inch bit. Placing ourselves in line with the gunner, Mel standing so that he could work the string with his foot, all was ready. Our three shots rang out simultaneously, the target fell, and with our smoking weapons still in hand, but held so as to be out of sight of the enemy, we all ran out to the target. We first placed our revolvers in our hip pockets, where they would be concealed by our coat tails, then picking up the much perforated stick, we engaged in a loud and animated conversation, from which our hearers were to learn that our last three shots had all taken effect. We walked back to our wagon with a swagger which could not possibly be mistaken for anything else than that we were not to be fooled with. We now unlimbered the gun, brought in the target and wound up the twine. The sun was still visible above the horizon.

Though we were highly elated with the success of our scheme, it was with a chilling sensation that we now perceived the horse-thieves bring out their guns and revolvers, and with what seemed to us as altogether unnecessary show, examine them carefully. They took out all the cartridges which were in the weapons and reloaded every piece, the Winchesters seeming to our fascinated gaze to consume an enormous number of the deadly missiles. However, these proceedings convinced us that they thought we were well armed and knew how to handle our weapons, and well they might, for our tactics would certainly have deceived any one. Their plan, we finally decided, was to slip over during the night and surprise us, get the mules, and commit any other atrocities their fiendish natures might suggest. But we should not sleep any that night. If they did attempt to come upon us unawares, we intended to meet them with a "game of bluff." We should be on the alert and suddenly confront them with our weapons presented, and as it would be a bright moonlight night, we trusted that the gleaming steel would put them to flight. Of the many ruses which we might have practiced, this was perhaps the boldest, most reckless and nonsensical one we could have hit on. But so far from seeing the danger of it, this plan grew in favor the more we discussed it. If we only had something with which to imitate the clicking of a revolver in being cocked we felt sure that our scheme would work. But we could not devise anything that would answer the purpose. Finally I remembered having read how one of the Fox sisters had hoaxed the public by making all kinds of queer noises with her big toe. I mentioned the fact to my comrades-in-arms, and they thought it quite possible that some of us possessed the same gift. We gathered our camp chairs around an upturned horse-pail, Jim and Mel facing each other and I facing the enemy, whom I could see by stooping a little and looking under the wagon. We removed our shoes and stockings and at once became a group of intensely interested experimenters. One knowing the depth of our emotions and seeing the look of anxious expectation on our faces could but have been touched with the pathos of our attempts to crack our toes with the clicking sound made in cocking a revolver. It was a complete failure. Sadly we put on our shoes, feeling anything but kindly toward the obdurate toes that refused to click. As we had our feet on the pail, these pedal contortions had been seen by the watchful enemy, but of course they could not have the faintest idea of our object.

We talked awhile longer, encouraging one another to believe that our plan would work without the clicking, then brought in the mules, tying them to the wagon, and made arrangements for the night. Shortly afterwards we retired to our schooner and cleared the deck for action. We close-reefed the wagon cover on the side toward the horse-thieves, so as to have an unobstructed view, then we raised the side boards about half an inch, making an aperture through which we could keep a watch, if we wished, without ourselves being seen. We then gave a little attention to our weapons in the way of polishing them up. The friction of the double-tree had already put a deadly glint on the wagon hammer. The monkey-wrench and bit, being new, required but little polishing to reflect the fatal moonbeams with a dangerous prodigality that boded ill to the enemy. For our own safety we handled our weapons very cautiously, remembering the many sad accidents from the careless use of firearms. Placing them where they could be easily reached in case of an attack, we lay down to rest, not intending to sleep.

For an hour the voices of the four men in the other wagon could be heard as they talked in low tones. The night was splendid, with a bright, silvery moon and myriads of soft, shining stars. In spite of our danger I fell to thinking about these mighty orbs that go whirling and careering through space. Did the starry world continue in extent on and on without end, each brilliant galaxy but the portal to some grander and more remote system of worlds, or was there a limit beyond which was a great, black, illimitable void? Again, would these great flashing suns and planets continue their orderly procession through space for all time, or would there come a season of chaos when they would all be reduced to one vast nebulous mass to again go through the process of world-making? And what place would man have in this grand succession of events? With such thoughts, and looking out into the glorious night, one could but be impressed with the splendor and majesty of existence.

The low tones of the enemy had gradually subsided, and the perfect silence which reigned recalled my thoughts to earthly things. I took a careful survey of the other wagon, but no one was to be seen. Our determination to keep awake made us drowsy, and the intervals between lifting our heads to look out grew longer and longer. Presently the men resumed their talk, and we all peered through the crack in the side of the wagon, but as no one appeared we soon lay down. For a long time I heard nothing but the munch, munch, munch of the mules as they cropped the grass within their reach. All at once the munching ceased. I was wide awake in an instant. I knew instinctively that the mules had had their attention attracted toward the other wagon. I nudged my companions and we all applied our eyes to the crack at the same instant. Our worst fears were realized. A lantern was burning brightly on a box about ten feet from the other wagon, and the four men were cautiously coming directly toward us. They all carried revolvers now, the barrels of which we could see flashing white in the moonlight. We hurriedly held a whispered consultation. Mel, whose forte was elocution, was to take command. When he gave the word we were to present arms and fire. If our first volley failed to check the enemy we were to fall back, paralyzed with fear, and let them do their worst. The horse-thieves were now within ten paces of our wagon. Mel, with all the assurance of one who has perfect

confidence in his oratorical powers, yelled: "Git!"
We all sprang up at the same time, and the surprised
cut-throats suddenly found themselves looking into
the shining barrel of a monkey-wrench, the cold
muzzle of a wagon-hammer and the relentless bore of
a 4-8 calibre bit. Our arms gained another signal
victory. The desperadoes whirled and fled tumultu-
ously for their wagon, into which they pitched themselves in a way that for a very brief instant presented
four pair of legs projecting perpendicularly into the
bright moonlight.

Proud of our success, we lowered our weapons,
laying them within easy reach of our now comparatively steady right hands. We had scarcely done so
when up raised the four men in the other wagon
accompanied by an ominous clicking, and we were
covered by guns of the most deadly pattern. Simultaneously there reached our ears the command:
"Lie down." They affected no oratorical flourishes,
but their impressive presentation of the cold facts in
the case swept away every vestige of the good impression made on our minds by the cunning and
eloquence of the defense. We threw ourselves down
with a precipitancy that made the bottom of the
wagon resound.

We were now at their mercy. While covered with
their guns, one of them could come over, first get the
mules, then return, reach over the side of the wagon,
revolver in hand, and perforate our loudly palpitat-
ing hearts at his leisure. We lay very quiet for a
long time. It was with deeply abused feelings that we

heard the mules resume their feeding as unconcerned as if the land were not overclouded with the smoke of battle, torn and convulsed with the shock of deadly strife! At length Jim, he of the wagon-hammer, mustered up courage to whisper:

"Boys, is any one hurt?"

Ascertaining that we had suffered no loss of life or limb, we cautiously lifted our heads and again applied our eyes to the crack. The first glance showed us the four men sitting where we had last seen them, the cruel guns held in the same position. With one accord we all raised our hands to the top of our heads to make sure no part of them obtruded above the side-boards. We lowered them with three distinct sighs of relief, perfectly satisfied for once that we had not been blessed with larger cranial developments.

It was evident by this time that we need not fear an immediate renewal of the attack. Beyond doubt they thought us armed and were determined not to let us "get the drop" on them again. The moon, however, would soon be down, when darkness would hide our movements. Deceived as they were, and unable to see our whereabouts, they would regard it as nothing less than suicide to make another advance.

A quarter of an hour later the moon disappeared. As darkness settled over the scene the lantern, which they had neglected to put out in their hasty retreat, lit up their surroundings while it served to throw us into deeper obscurity. They seemed to realize this, for suddenly a boot flew out of their wagon, as if propelled by an irresistible force, hit the lantern and knocked it about a quarter of a mile over in the direction of Del Norte. With the disappearance of the lantern, darkness prevailed and the hostile forces became invisible to each other.

We felt that we were saved. The enemy would not molest us under the uncertainties of darkness, and in the morning we should still keep up appearances. The obvious prominence of our revolvers, as they rested in our hip pockets, should show that we were ready for any onslaught, and they would be no keener to attack us than the day before.

With the first light of morning both camps were astir, if, indeed, they had not been all night. Broad daylight revealed us getting breakfast, moving about with protuberances under our coat-tails that looked like bustles which had slipped a little to one side. They would certainly indicate that we carried revolvers of enormous calibre. The enemy were also busy preparing the morning meal, two with revolvers buckled on them while the two Winchesters stood leaning against the wagon near by.

Just as we were sitting down to breakfast we were startled by one of the enemy calling out: "Say, over there, kill one of those antelope!"

We looked up to find them all excitement over a group of five antelope about one hundred yards distant looking at us with evident curiosity. They were noble animals, and the sight of them standing there in the bright morning light made our pulses thrill. They stood off to the rear of the wagons on a line about midway between them. Unconsciously both parties drew out toward the antelope. The shy creatures bounded off a little way, turned and watched us as before. We all made another advance. Again the antelope retreated and stopped. Both parties followed, coming within a few steps of each other. The antelope now dashed away out of sight, neither party having shown the least desire to display its marksmanship. We faced each other with looks of mutual contempt. With withering scorn their spokesman asked: "Why didn't you shoot one of them?"

"If we were a traveling arsenal," Jim retorted, with a sneer, "with all that ammunition you stuffed into it, we wouldn't have let an antelope get away."

"Ammunition, indeed!" the other replied with unguarded vehemence, "Do you call that ammunition?" taking from his pocket a handful of empty shells and tossing them in the air. "We've been out of cartridges," he continued, "for two days; but it's a downright shame for fine shots like you, with plenty of ammunition and good revolvers, to let those antelope get——

"Revolvers be hanged!" Jim interrupted, hotly, looking only to our honor in regard to the antelope, "Do you call that a revolver?" and he whipped out the wagon hammer with four pair of socks tied around one end of it.

This was too much for the gravity even of horsethieves and dyspeptics, and the true state of affairs having dawned upon us, roar after roar of laughter reverberated over the late battle field.

Explanations ensued as soon as our hilarity would permit. They were a party of divinity students of about our own ages, whom over-study had compelled to seek the mountains for rest and recreation. When they arrived at Colorado Springs, they had bought their outfit, including guns and ammunition jointly, had fitted themselves out with the tourist costume much in vogue at that time, and started for the San Juan Country in our wake. With the prodigality of inexperienced and eager marksmen they had shot away all their cartridges at prairie dogs, chipmunks, and anything else that came within range of their harmless fire. They had intended to replenish at Silver Cliff, but the belligerent miners had cornered the supply. They had driven into Silver Cliff about the time we drove out, staying there about two hours. The miners had told them all the pretty stories they had time to, and with the fatherly interest they take in all young credulous "tenderfeet," had especially warned them to be on the look-out for Alligator Bill and his two pals, Mosco Pete and Arizona Jack, the three worst horse-thieves and desperadoes in the West; and in order that they might know them had described us three innocents and our outfit to a dot. Their nerves were just right to make them keep a constant look-out for the dreaded horse-thieves. Of course they thought they had found them when they came upon us camped in the west opening of the pass. Both parties looked the worse from having faced the dust-laden wind that had blown all day from the south, so that our appearance, which, I venture to say, under ordinary circumstances would reassure the most timid, was then rather in keeping with the characteristic names we had received. But they were in the same predicament that we were, and had to stay there over night. They *knew* we were the terrible horse-thieves, and had followed the same course of reasoning that we had in regard to going on or turning back. Thinking that we were coming over merely to reconnoitre, and wanting to discourage all familiarity, and also to impress the fact upon us that they were well armed and knew just what sort of characters we were, they had given us the affront we had received, when we started to tender them the fruit. Their reloading, of course, had been done for effect, with empty shells.

Our wonderful marksmanship had completely deceived them, filling them with dread and terror. That we should attack them about midnight was a foregone conclusion. Our perfect silence they construed into the portentous calm that precedes the most terrific outbreak. As the time drew near for the inevitable massacre, their fears drove them to distraction. So sure were they that we should kill them to avoid trouble and the possibility of pursuit, that they finally concluded to put matters in such shape that we could not have even the shadow of an excuse for taking their lives. They got up, lit a lantern and proceeded to write out a bill of sale, conveying their horses, wagon and harness, and other personal property to us. As they would have to have our names to make the document of any worth they thought it would be

3

the proper thing to come over and present their visiting cards, hoping to be honored in return with those of Alligator Bill and his two confederates. With their cards, which our fears mistook for revolvers, in hand, they started over on their generous mission. They were just on the point of hailing us when our hostile demonstration made them forget all about the object of their visit and impelled them to flee for their lives. They had also raised the side boards of their wagon, and had seen us lay down our weapons, and on a sudden impulse born of despair had tried the effect of empty guns upon us. They had determined to hold the advantage thus gained until darkness came to their rescue. We in turn explained about the battery and the target. We had hoped to avoid having anything to say about the most ridiculous part of our proceedings, but one of them alluded to it, saying, "One thing greatly mystified and alarmed us, as we feared it was some incantation whereby you summoned the evil spirits to your aid—your marksmanship having already convinced us that you certainly had such aid —what in the mischief were you doing with your toes?"

We had to explain amid new explosions of laughter, mostly from our friends. But Mel about evened up by assuring them that if we spared their lives the bill of sale must be forthcoming.

Everything cleared up, we joined together and enjoyed a good breakfast, during which we planned to continue our journey in company for the remainder of the summer.

CHAPTER II.

By the time breakfast was over the sun was well up in the heavens. The sky was cloudless, but from some cause the atmosphere had become tinged with smoke, giving the sun a reddish cast, rather pleasant in its effect. We sought no further explanation of the phenomenon than that offered by one of our new friends, that the smoke of battle had not yet cleared away.

At nine o'clock we departed from the scene of our many miraculous escapes and began our journey through the desert, without any presentiments, or depression of spirits, though we were a little fearful of losing the way in the tangle of sage-brush that stretched out before us. Having some misgivings about water, we had taken the precaution to fill our two two-gallon water kegs just before starting.

When we got below the point where the water sank into the sand, five of us got out of the wagons and walked in the dry, sandy bed of the river. We thought it rather a novel proceeding to thus walk along over a great current of water that must be coursing its way beneath us. We stepped very lightly, somewhat apprehensive of a sudden giving way of our footing. Then we talked about how romantic it would be if

35

some of us should drop through and discover a dark, subterranean channel abounding in the marvelous, relieved here and there with rich deposits of gold and snug pockets of diamonds. At this stage of the picture, we walked more heavily, to enhance the possibility of breaking through. But as nothing of he kind occurred, we soon tired of walking and returned to the wagons. Mel concluded to try a sail in the students' schooner, while two of its crew shipped with Jim and me. We had all grown quite friendly. The night had demonstrated that the two parties had great respect for each other, and the fact that we had come through a common danger, as it were, made us feel very kindly toward one another.

The road proved to be much as the toll-gate keeper had said. At times we found it rather difficult to determine whether we were in or out of the way. It was only a continuous opening in the sage-brush, and as there were many other openings apparently similar, it required good judgment to decide which one to follow. We once discovered that we were out of the road by suddenly finding ourselves confronted with a thick tangle of sage-brush. Fortunately we had not gone far astray and had no difficulty in retracing our way to the road. Our wagons rolled along in the sand, which closed up in the wake of the wheels, leaving no more trace than if our wagons were indeed schooners upon "the trackless waste of waters." We made a mistake in not engaging some native to take steerage passage with us to steer us through the wilderness.

At noon we rested an hour, allowing the teams to feed on the grass, patches of which were encountered all along the route. After using what water we required for dinner, the remainder was given to the animals.

For two hours after dinner we pursued our way and had not come to the expected water. It was then three o'clock in the afternoon. We drove on for another hour and still no water. We had hurried our teams as much as possible, and must have traveled twenty-five miles at the least calculation. Could it be that we had mistaken the road? It was with growing anxiety that we pushed on for another hour, but only to meet the same disappointment. It was almost certain now that we were lost. For the last mile, clumps of sage-brush had been encountered here and there in the road. Still we pressed forward a mile farther, only to find the road completely overgrown and impassable. At six o'clock we were retracing our way, determined to make the most of the daylight yet remaining. At seven, the sun set like a great ball of fire, the atmosphere having grown more murky as the day advanced. The moon would give but little light through that dense medium, and it would require extreme watchfulness to keep the road in the dim light. Just as the last rays of daylight were fading away, our further progress was checked by a dense growth of the detestable sage-brush. Again we found our way back to the road, though with much difficulty. As the night would be cool we concluded to keep moving till we made our way out of this horrible labyrinth. It was not long, however, before we were again out of the road, nor could we find our way back this time. Again and again we thought we had found the right opening, only to run into the ubiquitous sage-brush at each new endeavor.

We were hopelessly lost, and all of us by this time were burning with thirst. We had not thought of eating, nor had we stopped to allow the teams to rest and graze. They too must be suffering for water, though not perhaps so severely as ourselves, for our fears undoubtedly aggravated our thirst. But it would not do to give up, and we continued our fruitless search for the road. At twelve o'clock we chanced upon a little clearing, with some dark object dimly outlined near the center of it. We made haste to investigate, and to our great joy found a half rotted down well curb which protected, or half protected, a veritable well of water in this dry and forsaken desert. I picked up a pebble and tossed it down the dark opening which the curb surrounded. An instant later and the agreeable splash of water reached our ears. The horses and mules had crowded up to the well along with ourselves. One of the ropes used in tethering out the horses was tied to the bail of a bucket, which was speedily let down into the well about twenty feet. It struck the water and Jim gave the rope a peculiar jerk; then we heard the bubbling, splashing sound of the water as the bucket turned over and filled. Hand over hand Jim drew the bucket up, the water trickling musically from its sides down into the well. As the bucket came to the surface we could see that it was filled with pure, sparkling water. Although our finer organizations made us suffer more keenly than the animals, yet they made us more humane, and we all insisted that the poor brutes be satisfied first. So Jim held out the water to the mules, which were pressing eagerly forward; but as their nostrils came to the rim of the bucket they started back with snorts of wildest terror, nearly upsetting the wagon in their mad efforts to get away from the water. When offered to the horses they showed even more fright than the mules, rearing and plunging frantically, and when quieted down stood shaking and trembling in a most pitiful manner. I had got a tin cup from our wagon, in the mean time, and being very thirsty was determined to have a drink. I first took a cup of the water and poured it over my hands, experiencing a cool and very pleasant sensation, for my hands were dry and feverish, and the water was cold. I then dipped up another cupful to drink, but no sooner did I raise it to my lips than a painful contraction seized my throat, an indescribable terror and loathing seemed to numb and shrink my body, chilling me with deadly horror. I dashed the cup and contents from me. It was the same with all the others; consumed with a raging thirst, intensified by sight of the water, yet unable to drink a drop. The well we had found in no wise reduced our danger of perishing for water.

Another danger now threatened. Since dark we had noticed to the west of us the glow-spots indicating the presence of fire, but so far away that we had apprehended no danger from that source. But for the past hour a strong wind had been blowing from the west, and the smoke and odor of burning sage-brush, or grease-wood, as it is well called, had been borne to our nostrils for some time. The flames were now in sight, and fanned by the rising wind were bearing directly toward us at an alarming pace. The heat and smoke were already disagreeable. The little clearing which we occupied would be no protection in that wilderness of raging fire. We could save ourselves by getting into the odious well, though we all had a holy horror of it, but the teams must be sacrificed unless they could outrun the fire, which was hardly probable. We quickly set them free from wagon and harness and tried to drive them away, but the poor frightened things could not be induced to leave their human friends.

We took off the wagon covers and thoroughly saturated them and also our blankets with water drawn from the well, and then spread them over the wagons, thinking that perhaps this might save them. It would have answered the purpose in an ordinary prairie fire, but we had our doubts in this case, as the grease-wood burns slower and with more intense and enduring heat. It would be hours before we should dare to come out of that terrible hole. We made up some bundles of provisions, and with ropes lowered them into the well, having first driven some stakes into the ground to which to tie the ropes. These were covered with dirt, to guard them against the fire. The boards of the curbing were torn off and laid over

the well, leaving a space just sufficient to admit us;
all was then covered with dirt so that the last one in,
by carefully adjusting a single board, would place a
dirt roof over our heads to protect us from the heat
and falling cinders. The well had a rough rock wall,
and with the ropes and parcels we should no doubt be
able to maintain a safe if not a comfortable position.

The smoke and heat had now increased to an in-
tolerable degree, and bidding good-bye to our poor
dumb friends, which were huddled together, snorting
and quaking with terror, we prepared to let ourselves
down through the aperture which had been left for
that purpose. It required great nerve on the part of
those who went in first, as they must, of course, be
nearest the mysterious water. Mel and one of the
students were the first ones to enter, after which the
rest of us were less reluctant to consign ourselves to
the disagreeable refuge. Jim, being the strongest,
was the last one in, as he could best arrange the
board that closed the opening, and shut us in from
the outer world—a world of raging fire.

Very soon we heard the fire sweep up to and around
the clearing, roaring and crackling like an artillery fusil-
lade. The frightful shrieks, almost human, of the
horses and mules chilled our very blood. Suddenly a
heavy fall overhead was heard, and a shower of dirt
rattled down upon us. The temperature becoming
uncomfortable near the surface, Jim begged those below to descend a little in order that he might seek a
cooler atmosphere. The rest of us were arranged in
groups of three. The three farthest down began to

lower themselves, but suddenly stopped with cries of horror. We all peered into the darkness below, and either from the fact that our eyes had grown accustomed to it, or from some peculiarity of the water, we distinctly saw four grinning skulls looking up at us from the bottom of the well, and we further perceived, with a creeping of the flesh, that they were alive and moved. This latter, however, proved to be a delusion caused by a ripple of the water. At Jim's renewed entreaties those below descended a few feet towards the ghastly objects beneath them; but again they were interrupted, this time by a portion of the wall caving in, the stones falling into the water with loud splashes. Quite an opening was faintly outlined in the wall. Fortunately some one had been thoughtful enough to put some candles into his pockets, and nearly all of us had matches. A light was soon struck, and a passage about three feet high and two wide was discovered. We clambered down and into the passage and the room into which it led, as quickly as possible. The apartment was ten feet square and nine high, an excavation, evidently the work of man. The four walls, roof and floor were bare dirt. The candle threw a pale, ghostly light around the room, revealing as its only furniture a strong box, or chest, which was wide open. A black velvet cloth concealed its contents. On lifting this there was displayed to our view the rarest collection of gold coins, diamonds and jeweled ornaments that ever dazzled the eyes of mortal man. A piece of parchment neatly folded was lying in one corner of the chest. On examination it was found to be written over with Spanish characters still plain and distinct. Mel and one of the students had made Spanish a study, and read the communication readily. Interpreted, it read as follows:

UNKNOWN LAND, Aug. 16th, 1803.

To Whom This May Come:

My name is Leon Espardo. I am a Spaniard and fifty-nine years old. For thirty years I have been a pirate, and this treasure has been accumulated through numerous fiendish acts of crime and bloodshed. Men, women and children I have murdered in cold blood. Many have gone down in scuttled ships after having been robbed of everything of value. The sea holds all my victims and they are legion. This ill-gotten wealth has become a curse to me, and for years I have been as active in trying to get rid of it as I was in gaining it. I could not bring myself to give it away, for it would entail upon the receiver the same misfortunes it had brought upon me. My first plan to dispose of it was to sink it in the sea. One dark night, with the assistance of three of my oldest followers, I took the chest in a boat and rowing a mile from my ship cast it into the water. But to our horror, for the others saw the occurrence, there came from all parts of the sea a most horrible array of my victims. I say most horrible, but that does not begin to express the loathsome spectacle—men, women and children in all stages of decomposition, ghastly corpses emitting a terrible odor and screaming at us in harsh, blood-curdling tones: "Take it away! take it away!" Pursued by the awful sounds, we hurried back to the ship, procured grappling hooks and returned to the place, easily discovered by the loud hideous disturbance that still prevailed. We recovered the chest, got it into the boat and under a frenzy of terror carried it back to the ship. I next tried to sink it in waters far distant from the scene of any of my atrocities, but the same foul, frightful assemblage raised their horrid din again, and we were glad to get back to the ship with the chest. I then tried more distant seas and rivers, but always with the same result.

But I must get rid of the accursed stuff. If the waters refused to receive it, then the land must become its burial place. With two teams and four trusty followers I have made my way from the Gulf of Mexico to this lone spot.

We first dug the well to supply ourselves with water, and afterwards excavated the room you are now in, to receive the treasure. When all was finished and the chest safely deposited underground, we filled our water barrels for the return trip. Then, unperceived by the others, I threw some of the blood cursed gold into the well to see what effect it would have on the water. I watched the men when they went to drink of it the last time. They would no sooner raise the cup to their lips than they would dash it from them with every expression of horror. As I wanted no living man to know where this accursed treasure was concealed, I offered the men wine drugged with a deadly poison. They drank of it eagerly and in a few moments later all four of them lay dead at my feet. I make my last visit to this room after their death. I shall ascend after walling up the opening of the passage, throw the bodies of the four dead men into the well, and make my way back to the Gulf alone.

My last words must be to warn the finder of this not to attempt to make use of the treasure. It will bring disgrace, misfortune and bitter suffering. It will fill his days with torture and rob his nights of rest. Sleeping or waking it will haunt him with demons and ghouls that never rest in their devilish torments. It will prove an eternal curse, burning and searing its way into his brain, filling it with a diabolical frenzy worse than the pangs of hell. By all you hold sacred in earth or heaven let the accursed stuff alone.

LEON ESPARDO.

We at once proceeded to select the most valuable gems and coins and stow them away in our pockets. There was a sufficiency for all; indeed, we should be compelled to leave the bulk of that glittering treasure hid away in that dismal hole, perhaps for ever. In the excitement of finding untold wealth, our thirst had somewhat subsided, and we had forgotten our terrible surroundings and the frightful experience we had had with the water. The touch of the jewels occasioned no unpleasant sensations, and we only felt elated over our discovery. As we fell to planning the great things we should do with our new found wealth, no thought of the warning was allowed to interfere with our bright pictures.

Three hours went by pleasantly before we thought of taking steps to regain the outer world, but as we should have to make our way out of the desert on foot, we could not tarry with our splendid dreams any longer. Jim taking the lead we began to climb to the top of the well, a distance of fifteen feet. Arriving at the covering, Jim essayed to push away the board he had last placed in position, but he could not budge it. It was the same with all the other boards. We were fastened in that odious hole with no means of escape. Had the curse of the ill-omened treasure already begun to work? Troubled with this thought we again repaired to the treasure room. It was suggested that we restore all the jewels and coins to the chest before we considered any plans for exhuming ourselves. It was contended, however, that our exit was hindered by the carcass of one of the mules or horses, and that we had heard it fall on the boards previous to our discovery of the treasure, and consequently the latter could not have had anything to do with it by virtue of any evil spell it might possess. This specious reasoning so relieved our minds that we managed to find room on our persons for a few more of the precious diamonds before we proceeded to discuss means of egress.

When we came to think of the matter calmly a very easy way out was hit upon. By removing the stones at the top of the wall we should have but a foot or so of loose sandy soil to cave down into the

well to make an opening through which we could
crawl out with but little difficulty. This plan worked
successfully.

It was in the dull grey of early morning when we
emerged from our living tomb. A scene of desolation
and gloom met our view. As far as we could see
there was nothing but a level stretch of black devas-
tation. Later we could see here and there little
wreaths of smoke curling upward from smouldering
embers where the sage-brush had been unusually large
and thick. Our wagons and supplies were reduced to
cinders. The horses and mules were dead, the body
of one of the horses lying across the well where it had
fallen in the last agonies of death.

Our first proceeding was to roll the dead horse out
of the way, after which we removed the boards and
drew up our parcels. For the first time since being lost
we felt like eating. Our stay in the cool, damp treasure room had allayed our thirst, and the pangs of
hunger now became uppermost. Fortunately our
packages consisted mainly of canned goods. We
opened a few cans of berries, eating the juicy fruit,
but carefully saving the liquor in which they were
preserved to drink later in the day. With some cold
meat and crackers we made out a very good breakfast. While we were eating the sun rose, looking like
a great ball of blood through the smoke which hung
over us like a pall. As we looked at the blood-
like orb no one said anything about our lately acquired wealth, but from the perfect silence which fell
upon us it was evident that each one was trying to

persuade himself that the vague, uneasy feeling which stole over him was in no wise due to the peculiar appearance of the sun.

Taking our bearings as well as we could we started on our journey back to the mountains. The snowy range had been plainly visible the evening before, but now nothing could be seen through the smoky atmosphere. At noon we drank the liquor we had saved from the morning meal and finished the cold meat and crackers. We now had three cans each of the fruit, or twenty-one cans all told. Of these we determined to eat but a can each per day, though we expected to reach the mountains the next day. As we had had two fair meals, we omitted supper, and lay down at night on the blackened ground to dream of sparkling streams and bounteous repasts.

The second morning the sun rose more blood-like than on the preceding day, and the smoke still hid the mountains from our view. The night found us apparently as far from our destination as when we started from the well. We lay down to more feverish dreams—more vivid visions of shaded brooks and luxuriously spread tables; keener disappointment in not being able to reach them. The third morning the smoke was heavier, the sun bloodier. At noon we consumed the last of our fruit—a very little remained, as hunger had driven us to eat more than we had allotted to each meal. It was evident by this time that we were merely wandering round and round; had it been otherwise, we should have long ago reached the mountains. After our last scant dinner the blood-like sun seemed to affect our brains. We talked blood, blood to drink, blood to quench our burning thirst. We had seen no living thing besides ourselves since we took leave of the horses and mules, yet we constantly talked of killing some wild animal whose blood we might drink. Again and again we repeated the fancy with but little variation. In the middle of the afternoon we came upon a human skeleton, the bones somewhat blackened by the fire which had passed over it. In examining it we found under the bones of the right hand a little heap of diamonds and gold coins and the charred remains of a leathern purse that had contained them. The jewels and coins were so similar to those in our possession that we could not doubt that they came from the same treasure pile. Some other unfortunate had found the treasure room and had endeavored to profit by his discovery, and here he lay at our feet a terrible witness to the folly of any such attempt. But instead of paying any attention to the ghastly warning, we appropriated the newly found gems and coins with a promptness and disregard of consequences that makes me shudder now as I think of it.

We rested here for some time. I was the weakest one of the party and would be the first, in all probability, to fall by the wayside. They had all been very kind to me, helping and encouraging me in many ways. As we rested we again fell to talking about the wild animal (soon to be caught, Jim assured me) the blood of which would revive our failing strength.

Then some one proposed that as soon as any of us became completely exhausted he should be killed and his blood drunk by the others. We all agreed to this. I was but dimly conscious of its import, and besides I felt my ability to keep up for a few days longer and we should find our way out by that time. Then one of the students suggested that we adopt a plan that should give the weakest an equal chance with the others. "We should draw lots," he said, "to determine which one of us should be sacrificed for the common good." This seemed the better plan to me, and it was surely just and right. I advocated it as well as I could. Jim, who was the strongest and bravest of us all, also favored it; indeed, there was but little opposition raised, and we adopted this last proposition nearly as readily as we had the first one. We further concluded to draw lots at once to see which of us was to be the first victim, who, on any of us becoming exhausted, would be put to the knife. Seven slips of paper, all blank but one, on which was written "Death," were prepared. One of the party had picked up the skull of the skeleton, and the slips of paper were now deposited in it and mixed up. The ghastly ballot box was passed around, each one drawing out one of the slips. Whoever drew the "Death" slip was doomed. Mine was blank. A painful silence ensued after the drawing. On looking around I discovered that Jim's face had blanched white, and I was sure it was he who had drawn the fatal slip. True, generous, noble Jim! He, so stout and strong; but his blood would be all the better for that, and I already thirsted for it. I

4

knew I could not struggle on for another half-hour, for I was already exhausted. Gentle, kind, patient Jim! I liked to dwell on his gentler virtues, for they encouraged my hope that he would yield submissively, and I should soon be drinking his blood. Had it been any of the others I should have feared their resistance at the time of sacrifice. Presently Jim held up the slip of paper on which was written "Death," disclosing himself to be the victim. His face was still white, but seemed resolute and determined. He let the slip fall to the blackened ground and said doggedly: "The man that drinks my blood'll be a hustler." It was also evident to my mind that if there was going to be any blood drunk, Jim would get his share of it, and a great fear possessed me.

Shortly afterwards we resumed our painful march. I kept away from Jim as far as possible, though heretofore he had helped and encouraged me more than any of the others. I was very fearful now that matters would take their natural course and the weaker fall a prey to the stronger, and I accordingly kept a close watch on Jim's movements. That night we slept but little. We had become suspicious, afraid, and watchful of one another, and we dared not sleep. All the next day these feelings increased and our sufferings grew more intense. A little before sun-down Jim had taken from his pocket a large clasp knife and was carrying it open in his right hand. I felt that I should become a victim before the great bloody orb, now sinking in the west, rose again. I made up my mind that when night came I should slip away from the others and try to find my way out of the desert alone.

Overcome with exhaustion and the vigils of the night before, it was no sooner dark than we all sank down, apparently to sleep. When I felt certain that all the others were sleeping I cautiously crawled away on my hands and knees. I had got but a little way when, looking back, I saw two half stooping forms coming after me. I at once rose to my feet and tried to run, but after a few staggering steps I fell, and a moment later two of the students were bending over me, knives in their hands and a fiendish light flashing from their eyes. They raised their knives to strike, but at that instant Jim came sweeping down upon us brandishing his knife. "Back, you dogs!" he cried hoarsely, and with one sweep of his arm he hurled their weakened bodies to the ground. I clung to his legs begging him to save me. The students slunk away, my protector glowering at them savagely. But now Jim was glaring down on me like a demon. His eyes were those of a savage beast and his lips curled away from his white gleaming teeth. I closed my eyes. He clutched my shoulder and shook me savagely. Again I looked up into his face, but it had lost its demoniacal expression, indeed, it looked kindly and jolly as he said: "Come, get up, old boy; dinner's ready and you've had a long sleep."

Yes, it was all a horrible dream. Awake all the night before, I had succumbed to nature and fallen into a troubled sleep almost immediately after getting into the wagon, its easy, noiseless motion through the yielding sand being conducive to slumber. The red appearance of the sun in the morning, the smoky atmosphere, the talk about the underground channel and of finding diamonds and gold, the fear of getting lost and the fact that I had grown very thirsty during my sleep had done all the rest. A glance at my very lean pocket-book would account for my desire for diamonds, and my clinging to them so tenaciously in the face of such warnings is explained by the fact that in dreams we lose the moral sense altogether, which also explains my greedy willingness to drink my companion's blood. And I trust it will be borne in mind that the more active and exacting the moral sense is, in waking hours, the wilder and more reckless it is liable to be when freed from its restraints by sleep.

We had arrived at a clear stream, threading its way through a grassy valley. My comrades had prepared dinner, kindly allowing me to sleep till it was ready. The mules and horses, which I never expected to see again, looked fat and sleek and the very picture of content, as they fed on the grass, fresh and green. The boys were alive and jolly. A delightful breeze was supplying invigoration and good cheer in a most wholesome and luxurious way. The atmosphere had cleared up, the sun was shining brightly, the distant mountains to east and west lifted their purple silvery heights to laughing blue skies, and life never seemed brighter or fairer than when we sat down to as good a repast as any I had seen in my dreams.

CHAPTER III.

THE LOVERS' SPRING.

DINNER disposed of, we were soon under way again. A quarter of a mile from the stream the grassy strip merged into the monotonous sage-brush, but the road was well defined and easily followed.

We were in high spirits, the effect of the champagne-like atmosphere in reality, but to all appearance we had undergone a change of state, for there was nothing in our surroundings to account for the intense joy we felt in the mere fact that we were alive. On the contrary our environment was the very abomination of desolation—a sandy, sage-brush plain —and yet our internal state was as perfect as if we had been transported to the garden of Eden itself. I am inclined to think that this is the site of the Adamic paradise, and that the cherubim and sword are but typical of sand and sage-brush.

Towards sundown, as we came to no stream or ranch, we began to fear that we should have to make a "dry camp." This would be no great hardship, as we had no apprehensions of being lost and we should reach the Rio Grande by noon the following day. However, camping without water is inconvenient, and we should travel late rather than stop before we found it.

The sun was now setting in true royal splendor. Two banks of clouds, one of light, fleecy masses, the other of darker hue, near the horizon, appeared to be vying with each other in a display of gorgeous coloring. The exquisite tints of orange and red, exhibited by the lighter mass, seemed matched against the magnificent purple and gold of the darker one. It was grand and beautiful beyond description, as all sunsets are. And what is it that gives to these airy, ephemeral visions their transcendent charms? We all delight in them and yet they are but a chaos of rich colors. Is it that they furnish to the mind a richness and plenitude of material which the fancy may build into shapes and pictures to suit itself, or do they merely speak of a glory and sublimity beyond the world, where still more splendid hues and far more luminous material are wrought into enchanting forms of beauty, to delight the spirits of the blest? But is there any absolute beyond? We have already come through the valley of shadows, crossed the Delectable Mountains and drunk in the ecstacies of this heavenly, balmy region, and now before us we see in cloudland still more entrancing visions of loveliness beckoning and luring us on, and will it not ever be thus now and hereafter?

We traveled on till nine o'clock, when fortunately we came to a large tank surmounted by a wind-mill. There was no habitation near, and we supposed the tank and well had been erected in that lonely place to water stock. The tank was empty, but the well afforded an abundance of water, so that we camped very comfortably.

By the middle of the following forenoon we had reached prairie land and were rolling along on a good hard road at a lively rate. We had been told of the pleasures of a swim in the Rio Grande, and the fine sand and dust of the regions through which we had been driving made us literally itch for the luxury of a bath; besides, we were all good swimmers, and anticipated no little fun when we arrived at the beautiful river. At ten o'clock we could see the line of trees that marked the course of the river through the San Luis valley, and an hour later we had reached the Mecca of our desires. We were at first disappointed to find* the river broad and shallow, dashing along over and around great boulders. But surely we should find deep pools before we journeyed far up the stream, and so it proved. We soon came to a secluded spot that would make a splendid place to camp, and near by a deep, still pool that would make a famous place to swim. Hardly waiting to "picket out" the teams, we all rushed down to the river and engaged in a lively race to be the first one in, with the result that we all made the plunge nearly at the same time; and what an icy plunge it was, and with what utterly crazy haste we got out again. With gasps like the exhaust of a locomotive we vigorously applied our Turkish towels, and after having donned our clothes the glow of warmth and good feeling we experienced convinced us that a swim in the Rio Grande was all that was claimed for it, but that was our first and last swim in the noble stream. Two days later, at noon, we were camped near the river many miles above Del Norte, and but a few miles from Wagon Wheel Gap.

We were now in the mountain fastnesses. Everywhere were great rocky masses towering upward to the skies. There were numerous caverns, cañons, gorges and valleys inviting exploration, and we decided to camp a day or two in this picturesque region.

Just as we were sitting down to dinner a horseman rode up. With true Western hospitality he invited himself to dinner before we had time to extend the invitation. We were only too glad to exchange the best our larder afforded for the experiences of any of these "old timers" such as our guest appeared to be. He had been up to "the Gap" and was on his way home, about ten miles farther down the river. He had a fund of information and anecdote of the region from Alamosa up to the San Juan country. He had been an eye witness to a tragic event that had occurred a little over a year before, and very near the place where we were then camping. We had heard the story before, but to have it told by one who could vouch for every particular was a treat we had not expected. In a valley to the west of us and probably a quarter of a mile distant stood a deserted house, which, two years previous, had been the home of John Andrews, a well-to-do stockman. He had an amiable wife and three children. His sister, Jennie Andrews, at the death of their mother, their only surviving parent, had given up the school she had been teaching in Illinois and had come west to make her home with her brother.

The fair Jennie was soon besieged by suitors for her hand, but the contest quickly narrowed down to two contestants, Mose Skein and Edward Laird. Skein was a broncho breaker in the employ of Mr. Andrews. He was handsome, honest, brave and free-hearted, and the young lady's preference. But Edward Laird, a neighboring ranchman, was "well-heeled," that is, owned a drove of cattle, a good ranch and a number of horses, and was Mr. and Mrs. Andrews' choice. The young lady, however, had a will of her own, and could not be persuaded nor coerced into accepting the rich lover. Skein had been discharged by Mr. Andrews on a mere pretext, for no other purpose than to discourage his suit. He was forbidden the house, but the lovers met occasionally at a dance or social gathering. Then they designated a trysting place where they met more frequently, and often left letters for each other.

Laird, having failed to win the lady's love by fair means, had not hesitated to resort to foul, in getting rid of his successful rival. Mose being in love and "all broke up," had not, at once, tried to get work, when he found himself out of employment. He stayed at Del Norte most of the time, and like young men of his social disposition out of work, was frequently found having a good time with the "roughs" of the vicinity. A number of horses had been stolen in the neighborhood, and some one had fastened suspicion upon Skein, who, it may be said, was perfectly innocent. But such evidence had been laid before the vigilance committee that it warned Skein to quit the country inside of twenty-four hours under penalty of death. This warning was a leniency not usually shown by the committee, and had been secured with difficulty by warm personal friends of Mose, who could not bring themselves to believe in his guilt. Mose, while knowing that he was wrongly suspected, yet knew that his best policy for the present was to "make himself scarce" for a few months. Laird, believing that Skein would not leave without first seeing his sweetheart and that he could not accomplish this in the specified twenty-four hours, had gathered together some of the vigilants and set them to watch the premises of Mr. Andrews. On the second night after the edict Skein had ridden to within half a mile of the Andrews ranch, tied his horse in a grove of trees and was making his way on foot to the trysting place, when he was suddenly halted by the vigilants and commanded to "throw up his hands." Skein, however, trusting to the darkness, had made a break for life and liberty. No shots were fired, for the men had noticed what Skein in his excitement had not, that he fled up a cañon which terminated in abrupt walls and from which no human being could escape except through the outlet which they held. At the further end of the cañon was a pool or large spring remarkable for the fact that no bottom had ever been discovered to it. The vigilants had immediately given chase, and, closely pursued, Skein had been brought to a standstill on the edge of the pool. Knowing that death by hanging awaited him if he fell into the hands of his relentless pursuers, he had preferred death by drowning. He plunged into the spring and sunk and sunk until no trace of the dead body was ever seen.

The death of her lover had nearly killed Jennie Andrews. So great was the shock that for a week her friends despaired of her life. Then she rallied somewhat and to the surprise of every one had favored the suit of her rich lover. A few weeks later her engagement to Laird was announced and friends were invited to the wedding, which was to take place on the 16th of August, just two months from the day on which her lover had drowned himself. Many invitations had been given and a joyful time was anticipated. The wedding eve arrived, and many guests, among whom was the narrator, had assembled at the Andrews home to witness the ceremony and to join in the festivities of the occasion. The bride elect had been arrayed in her wedding dress, and a few minutes before 8 P. M., the hour set for the solemn rite, had asked to be left alone in her room. The bridesmaid withdrew. A few minutes after 8 o'clock, becoming impatient at the young lady's delay, they rapped at her door, but received no response. The door was then pushed open; a window was up and Jennie was missing. On making this discovery several hurried outside. A white form was seen flitting up the cañon towards the bottomless pool. Her brother and lover, divining her intent, put forth all their speed to intercept her and prevent her self-destruction. But she reached the pool fifty yards in advance of her pursuers, and with a wild, mocking laugh that chilled them with horror, the loyal girl that preferred the arms of Death to those of a selfish, cruel husband, plunged into the dark waters. Our guest, who had closely followed the brother and lover in their pursuit, had heard the mad laugh and seen the fatal plunge. The body was never recovered, as that dark, frightful, bottomless pool never gave up its dead.

Laird, suffering bitter disappointment, and knowing himself a double murderer, had become insane, and from his wild ravings enough had been gathered to disclose that it was he who had driven Skein to his death by his misrepresentations to the vigilants. The walls of a mad-house in the far east alone protected him from the vengeance of those friends of Skein, of whom our informant was one, who had so warmly defended him before the vigilance-committee. The Andrewses, conscience-stricken at their own part in the tragedy, soon moved far away from the scene of the sad affair. But surely distance will not enable them to forget the sweet young sister whom they helped to drive to her death.

Rumor said that the "Lovers' Pool," so it had been named, was haunted. Our guest, "for himself," believed it. "I aint no skolar," he said, "nor no grate shakes for nateral ability, but twenty years in these diggins has pounded a lot of hard horse sense into my head, if I do say it myself, and I'm not likely to see ghosts in my mind. If I war I'd receive a visit once and a while from the spirit of Dan Cable, who allowed one day that I lied about some calves of mine which he had branded. As Dan got up, he drew his pop, but I got the drop on him and his funeral took place next day. The boys all said it war far and squar and as purty shootin as they ever seed. Then Bill Wright, down to Del Norte, got huffy over a game of poker and wan't going to be sociable, declined pint blank to drink with me when I called all the boys up to drink in Dave Blank's s'loon. Well, it come to shootin and Bill war buried that afternoon. Some of the boys kicked and I war a'rested, leastwise I war taken before 'the gang' for exzaminashun. But ole Jedge Blackstone got up and jest give 'em law from his finger tips. He adjudicated that if social customs war going to be vierlated and tromped under foot we might as well invite anarky and lawlessness to roost with us, and dispense with the dignity and majesty of the law to once, and that when gentlemen refused to drink with each other every loyal citizen war bound to protect himself. Ther boys jest wilted under that and I wan't molested no more. Then ther war Ike Steel, and well named he war, for he'd steal cattle and butcher 'em, burning or burrying the hides so the brands wouldn't give him away. But once we caught him skinnin a steer with Andrews's brand onto it. We hustled him off to some trees, and I've never denied that I put the noose around his neck, throwed the rope over a limb, got on my bronco, wrapping the end of the rope around my saddle horn, and set my pony to bucking in a way that broke the thief's neck at about the second pitch he made, and I am shure that war more gentler than to strangle him by degrees. But none o'ther spirits ever bothered me. No sir, I've no spookish squeamishness in my make up, but I've seed sights around that ther spring that has made me a better man and made me believe in spirits and heaven—yes, and made me feel awful sorry about Bill Wright. What I've seed with my own eyes's nuff to make me jine meetin. I've seed them two poor innocent lovers a sitting by that pool, she with her wedding dress all white and a long shiney veil, and Mose in his brown canvas coat and leather schaps with the water a tricklin off the leather fringes, and their faces shining awful white in the moonlight. I'd see 'em only for a little while, then Jennie'd put her arms around Mose's neck and together they'd disappear in that awful deep spring.''

At the word ''moonlight'' Mel and I had exchanged glances. Further inquiries elicited the fact that it was on cloudy, moonlight nights that the spirits of the lovers had been seen. By one whose mind had received the shock of seeing the young lady drown herself, patches of moving moonlight would be easily mistaken for the forms of those so vivid in his fancy. Still, as his superstition made him a better man we had no desire to disabuse his mind. After he had ridden away we fell to discussing whether we did right in making no effort to show him the error of his belief in ghosts. It was a question if we should not have insisted upon convincing him of the truth that the ghosts were in his mind—even if his moral nature did suffer by it? Then I extended the question to Christianity itself. Was it not a mere ghost story which had been long and successfully employed to induce the superstitious to live better lives? Six of the party were emphatic in denying that it was any such story, and I was glad to concede that if it were, it was the grandest triumph of human reason, and must rank foremost as a civilizing and humanizing institution, that it had been essential to moral progress, and that only harm could result in any attempt to suddenly disillusionize its devotees.

After dinner we started out according to the directions given us by the erstwhile bold, bad ranchman, "Bill Mundy, Esq.," as he gave his name, to find the Lovers' Pool. It proved to be in a wild, lonely gorge, which at no place was over twenty feet wide. Pine and spruce trees grew along its sides close to the walls. In places high up over our heads, where a crack in the rock had admitted a scant supply of earth, a thrifty pine would be seen growing apparently out of the solid rock. Here and there were great fissures and crevices where the mighty forces that had upheaved these stupendous hills had split the rocks with reports that must have far exceeded the most terrific peals of thunder.

The pool, owing to the deep shade thrown upon it by the towering walls of the cañon, looked dark and mysterious. No eye could penetrate more than a few inches below its placid surface. It was nearly round, about ten feet in diameter, and, as has been said, of unknown depth. Two posts had been set in the ground eight feet apart, and near the edge of the pool. To these had been wired a stout pole after the manner of building pole fences in the west, which was probably intended as a protection against the intrusion of stock. Like other deep springs in that region, the water was rather warm and of a somewhat brackish taste. Mel had leaned far over the pole trying to peer into the water. Jim banteringly asked him to try a drink of it. "No," Mel had answered, "I'll have nothing to do with it." Just at that instant one of the posts, which had rotted almost away in the damp earth, snapped asunder and Mel was precipitated headlong into the pool. The accident immediately following his words, and never dreaming but that drowning was optional with those who plunged into the pool, we all broke into a loud laugh. Then as Mel did not instantly reappear an awful silence fell upon us. Another breathless instant and the wildest consternation seized us. Still madly hoping that Mel was playing a trick on us we gazed eagerly at the pool, now settling again into its cruel placidity, for some moments before we made a move. But what could we do? We were utterly powerless to save him, or to recover the body. Jim hurried back to the wagons and got our ropes and lines and a piece of heavy wire with which we made a grappling hook, and every endeavor was made to recover the body. Surely our companion could not be thus suddenly swept from our sight forever. Could I be dreaming again? For a moment I felt a deep feeling of relief. Surely it was one of my terrible nervous dreams. But no, there was the pool, the boys with white, grief-stricken faces, the cañon, the trees—all convinced me that I was awake and Mel's loss a terrible reality.

We may mistake our dreams for realities, but we cannot mistake our waking impressions for dreams. For a half-hour we continued working to recover the body before we gave up in despair. Then we beheld a sight which for once and forever swept away all skepticism that we may have entertained as regards the ranchman's story of the spirits. We had just raised up from our knees, as we had been kneeling around the pool in our fruitless labors, when there, not over fifteen feet distant from us, stood the form of Mel. The face was of a deadly pallor, and locks of wet hair hung over the marble brow. The countenance was pinched and rigid; the glassy eyes were wide open and staring straight into the water at which the rigid upraised right arm and hand also pointed. Noiselessly the spectre glided to the brink of the pool and silently disappeared into its dark depths.

Our grief was now transformed into an awful horror. I could but feel that this apparition was a spiritual visitant, calling on me to plunge into the fatal pool and join my cousin. The others also felt that they had received a special summons to the spirit world. In our terror and agitation we did not, we could not, think calmly. We acted wholly on impulse and in a condition of mind bordering on frenzy. This ocular demonstration of that in which we had always disbelieved unbalanced us. Our complete liberation from superstition proved our bane, for had we believed in ghosts, we should have been, undoubtedly, better prepared to act rationally in such an emergency. We were but a few moments in resolving

6

on suicide. Self-destruction, in the face of what had just occurred, lost all its disagreeable features. It could not be wrong, for we were obeying a supernatural summons which we dared not resist. It was speedily arranged that in solemn procession we should enter the other world through the portal of the dark, treacherous pool. Allowing four minutes interval between each plunge we should follow one after the other in taking the fatal headlong leap. I was in no wise loath to take the lead in this justifiable suicide, and without a moment's hesitancy I sprang head-foremost into the pool. I sank rapidly for several feet, then came the wild uncontrollable desire to live. I had always had great will power, and now I thought by sheer force of will I would overcome the spell of the water that had so relentlessly destroyed others. I essayed to rise again to the surface, but a weight like that of a mountain mercilessly held me down. But I was determined and lunged frantically. Thank heaven, I rose as rapidly as I had sunk. But what was my surprise to come up in a strange place—a lovely little grotto with a soft, subdued light, but from the fact that my eyes had been shut while in the dark waters I could see distinctly immediately on coming to the surface. There was the ghost in the very unangelic act of wringing out a pair of socks. The truth broke upon me in a flash. My first sensation was a thrill of exquisite pleasure at the thought that the lovers—Mose and Jennie—had escaped after all. My second sensation at the thought that I myself had escaped was also a thrill of pleasure, but not so intense as the first one. Then I was glad to find Mel alive, even though he had played such a joke on us. His face was still splotched with white, and an open box of Lily White lying near him, which he had found in the grotto, explained the corpse-like appearance of the ghost. The cosmetic had suggested to Mel the idea of whiting up and playing ghost. Its presence there also indicated that the grotto had had a lady tenant, and who could it have been but Jennie Andrews? But I had no sooner taken in the situation than I, too, wanted to play a joke on the boys, and my third sensation had been one of exhilaration at the thought of the fun we might have with the others as they came through. They would plunge in at such an angle as to come up first against that portion of the mountain which divided the two pools and which extended about five feet below the surface of the water. Then they would want to live, think they had great will power, and would lunge forward in their struggles to rise. The depth and buoyancy of the water was such that when any one of them started to rise he would come up with a rapidity that would shoot him out of the water half his length. I had come up that way and so near the edge of the pool that I had put out my hands and easily prevented myself from sinking back under the water.

Mel and I hurriedly whitened up our faces, and cross-legged tailor fashion sat down on the edge of the pool. We then set our features into corpse-like rigidity, and fixing our eyes with a stare at the water, awaited developments. They came.

The next arrival from the vale of tears was one of the students, who, of course, came up right in the face of two ghastly objects. With the swiftness and energy of terror and desperation, he dealt me a blow between the eyes with his right hand which sent me sprawling over backwards, while he buried the fingers of his left hand in Mel's hair and holding on with the grip of a drowning man, pulled him off into the water, where they fought and clawed each other in a most shameful way for two persons who had just crossed the threshold of the better world. Finally I got them out of the water and separated, but not in time to receive the next arrival, another of the students, who, in a dazed sort of a way, grasped the situation. Then we whited up again, and the four of us took positions as before, only far enough back to be out of harm's way. Another of the students came up promptly on schedule time. In his fright he did not attempt to prevent himself from sinking back under the water, and of course got only one good look at us before he disappeared. But that was sufficient, and in his face we read the wish of his heart, that he might not rise again; but in a second up he came. Then the play of his countenance was the interesting feature of the occasion. We sat perfectly motionless and as relentless as fate. It was evident that he was doubtful as to whether he was dead or alive, and then, convinced that he must be dead, he was more doubtful as to which place he had arrived. He would blink his eyes and then rub them, like one waking up from a deep sleep, all the while wavering between the desire to pull himself out and the impulse to try to drown himself again. It was certainly a matter of the most profound wonder to him, when his senses finally told him that he must be alive, that he was confronted with the corpses of his four companions who had preceded him. While he was yet in his quandary another arrival from the mundane sphere announced himself in the abrupt manner that seemed to be the correct thing in making the transit. It was the only remaining student. He repeated the manœuvres of the other. The two would be somewhat reassured with a look at each other. Then in doubt they would gaze at us, then turn their eyes on each other again with inexpressible solemnity. The great fun of it was that we dared not laugh, while the desire to do so nearly killed us.

But we had to cut our fun short and get them out in time to receive Jim. They were treated to a coat of the whiting, and a formidable array of six most horrible looking ghosts awaited the last pilgrim. And we waited a long time. We sat there with our faces fixed and immovable until we nearly had the lock-jaw. The fact was that Jim had had twenty-four minutes in which to collect his scattered senses and to allow his better judgment to assert itself. No doubt he too had approached the pool with a half notion of throwing himself in it; but there would be no need to hurry. There were no others waiting, no pressure from behind, as it were, and the last two students confessed that but for what those behind them would think, they would not have had the courage to take the fatal leap. Of course the longer Jim tarried the less likely he would be to follow us. In short, he had finally concluded not to make his exit from the world just at present. This, no doubt, was highly creditable to his common sense, but it did not seem to be doing the right thing by the rest of us, and we should just bide our time, and that night scare him to death or into incurable madness. Jim, we were sure, did not understand the true state of affairs. The most noise that had been made was when Mel and the student were struggling in the water, and not a sound had reached the others, who afterwards came through. After planning many different diabolical schemes that promised an uproariously hilarious time, we began to fear that they might terminate more seriously than we wished. In the face of all that had occurred that day, Jim would be in a condition to be easily scared into fits. We finally settled on the following plan: After Jim had retired for the night we should put on our whiting, steal into camp, rekindle the fire, so as to make a strong light, and then silently proceed to prepare our suppers. The fire would arouse Jim, who would not sleep very sound that night. He would raise up and be somewhat frightened to see so many cadavers in camp. We could very safely grin back at his wondering gaze, for the great gashes thus revealed in the fearfully white faces made them look all the more ghastly. We even practiced on one another, both to make our grins more effective and to regain our wonted mobility of features, which had become somewhat impaired by the long continued rigidity, we had just imposed on them. As we should be employed in cooking, Jim would have time to grasp the situation while in doubt as to whether he was awake or asleep. The odors of boiling coffee and frying meat would indicate that we were of the human order of beings rather than of the celestial or infernal. It would dawn upon him gradually and safely that by some means we had escaped and were alive and hungry.

From the grotto a crevice led out to the cañon about twenty-five yards below the pool. At the entrance it was not more than eighteen inches wide and was screened by a dense growth of tall pine trees. Above these trees the long slender crack did not look to be over five or six inches wide and no one would have thought that back of those trees was an opening which would admit a man. Mel had slipped around this way and played ghost to a small but very appreciative audience. When we came out into the cañon we found Jim had returned to the wagons and had taken all the fishing tackle with him.

We followed up the valley until we came to another cañon, into which we penetrated probably two hundred yards. A pocket match-safe had brought some matches through the water in good condition, and we soon had a rousing fire, by which we dried our clothes and made ourselves comfortable. We should have to wait about four hours before we could have our ghostly supper pantomime. We employed the time in speculating about how Skein and his sweetheart had outwitted their persecutors. Skein, no doubt, had intended to commit suicide, and we rejoiced at the thought of how surprised and happy he must have felt on coming up in the grotto safe and secure from his enemies. He had then made his escape known to Jennie, and they had planned their revenge on Laird and the Andrewses. They had been more successful, perhaps, in carrying it out than they had intended. Jennie had known just where she would land when she made her bold plunge, and we thought her pretty brave, even if she did know. She had probably secreted provisions where Mose could get them and carry them to the grotto, and so provided for their subsistence while they lingered a few days to personate their departed spirits. Finally they had made their way to some other portion of the State, got married and were living happily, as they deserved. It was just delightful to think that we alone shared this truly lovely secret with Jennie and Mose. We ventured that Jim would have been willing to commit suicide to have learned this charming sequel to the ranchman's story a half-day sooner. We did **not** exactly approve of our heroine using lily-white, but we forgave her in consideration of the fun we had had with the box of it she had so kindly left us. And then there was more fun yet to be had with it.

About an hour after dark we made up our faces and moved toward the seat of operations. We had not neglected to keep a watch on Jim's movements to guard against his driving off and leaving us a long walk **on** our hands, as the Irish would say. As we drew near the clump of bushes that screened our approach, we suppressed our chucklings, though with difficulty. When we got within the bushes we could see the camp and surroundings. Our victim had not retired as we expected. A fire was burning brightly, near which Jim sat, the very picture of sorrow and woe. The tears were coursing freely down his cheeks, and the heavy sobs which he in nowise tried to restrain, completely unnerved us. For the first time we realized how grieved Jim must feel over our supposed loss. The tears that started to our own eyes did not promise much for hilariousness. We all slipped down to the river and washed the powder off our faces, using about as much salt water as fresh. We were still in a dilemma, however, as we did not know how to introduce ourselves in the face of such deep sorrow. We finally decided that we should all step out into the light, laughing, Mel at the same time assuring Jim that we were not ghosts, but bone and flesh and appetite, and that we had been saved by diving under a rock and coming up in a grotto on the other side.

When we came back, Jim, in his great loneliness and grief, was sobbing harder than ever. We carried out the programme, only we were all crying, and Mel said with a quavering voice:

"Why, Jim, we ain't hurt."

CHAPTER IV.

THE FIRST MESSAGE.

JIM's surprise and joy can better be imagined than told. It was a very happy party that sat down to a late supper that night in the wilds of the Rocky Mountains. A great fire of pitch-pine logs burned cheerfully, but the experiences of the day and the manner of our home-coming, so to speak, had rather sobered us, and our happiness was of a quiet, undemonstrative kind. Sleep was out of the question. We talked over the occurrences of the day, and our conversation soon drifted into a controversy over the problem of death and the mystery of the hereafter. Little we knew that we were on the eve of a discovery that would throw much light on these subjects.

It was three o'clock in the morning before we finally retired, and the middle of the following forenoon before we awoke. There had been no occasion for early rising, however, as the animals were our only care, and being within reach of water they could live sumptuously for a week on the rich grass in which they were tethered.

By eleven o'clock we had breakfasted and were ready for a ramble through the mountains. Just as we were starting out we met a mountaineer with a gun over his shoulder and a revolver and knife in his belt. He greeted us with a good-natured "Hullo," and forthwith volunteered the information that they had a new baby up at his "diggins." "My ole woman's mammy," he continued, "has been visiten us nigh onto a week and between her'n the kid I'm driv out on a hunt to find peace and quiet, and I'm bound to have 'em if I have to fight ba'r for a week. Nothen like a tus'l with a bar to quiet and soothe nerves. Ben Johnson sed he seed fresh tracks over in Owl Gulch yesterday, and from their size 'lowd 'twas the biggest bar ever been in these here mountains. Hope 'tis. Bigger the bar, bigger the soothe. S'pose you fellers air looking for sights. There's a cave, and a mighty fine one, just bey'nt them thar rocks," and he pointed his gun at some detached pieces of mountain about a quarter of a mile up the river. On assuring him that a cave was just in our line, he advised us to get some pitch-pine torches, and also a rope to let ourselves down into the "cellar of the cave," as he called it. After more specific directions in regard to the cavern, he went on his way to find the "big bar" where his weary nerves would be at rest and his mother-in-law cease from troubling. We could but comment on the singular beauty of the hunter. He was probably forty-five years old, though he looked not over thirty. Six feet tall, and with a form perfectly proportioned, his strength must certainly have been marvelous. A frank, open countenance, a clear white and pink complexion, regular features, lit up by large, intensely black eyes, soft and gentle in their expression, formed a face as handsome and as pleasing as one could wish to see. Add glossy black hair and whiskers, and you have Sim Pardee, the hunter. His clothing had been brown duck, but was now black and shiny, and patched until but little of the original garments remained.

We were not long in reaching the cave. We crawled into it on our hands and knees, and found a very ordinary cavern consisting of one large room. Near the center of this apartment, however, was a round, black opening with a six-foot log thrown across it. This was the entrance to a perfect wonderland of stalactitic grandeur. We first tied knots about a foot apart in our rope and then fastened it to the log which spanned the pit. By means of this rough rope ladder we descended to the lower cavern. On lighting our torches, which blazed out instantly, we found ourselves in the midst of a perfect forest of glittering and sparkling stalactites and stalagmites. The coloring ranged from dazzling white, through delicate pink and yellow, to dark brown. All kinds of grotesque formations surrounded us; and yet some of these formations were not so grotesque either. In one place was the statue of a man only a little less perfect than the most skillful sculptor could have produced, and not far away was the form of an elephant as natural as life, though not nearly so large as a baby elephant. I could but feel that if such blind, lifeless agents as limestone and dripping calcareous water could thus shape such perfect forms it was no matter of wonder that the active, potent forces of electricity, heat and sunlight should naturally produce plants, animals and human beings.

Grand and curious though it was, we tired of it as soon as we found another dark opening similar to the one through which we had just descended. Our desire now was to explore its depths in hopes that we might find still greater wonders, going from glory to glory, though by an altogether different route from the one generally supposed to be the right one. Jim and two of the students returned to the outer world and procured a log which we laid across the pit. The last one to descend from the upper room had untied the rope, and by doubling it over the log was enabled to let himself down safely. As we could throw the rope up over the log again, it was pulled down to assist in our further explorations. Our rope was about eighty feet long and we concluded first to tie it around Jim, who had volunteered for the purpose, and lower him down into the pit. When down about ten feet he gained a footing on the floor of a passage which seemed to lead down into the bowels of the earth. Telling us to let out the rope slowly and steadily, he proceeded to make his way carefully down the incline. Jim soon called back to make the rope fast to the log and come down. He cautioned us to hold carefully to the rope, and to put out our torches, as it was already "lit up by electricity or something." We descended in such a hurry that only good luck saved us from accidents. On reaching Jim we found that we were ten or twelve feet above the floor of a magnificent room lit up by a phosphorescent moss-like sub-

stance on its rock ceiling. By some freak of percolation
the walls were hung with the richest stalactite tap-
estry, which fell from ceiling to floor in such natural
folds that we momentarily expected to see them
undulate in the currents of air that played freely
through the cavern. From the flora-like formations
scattered about the apartment we named it the Conservatory of the Gods. Trees, flowers and shrubs
were imitated to perfection. A brook of clearest
water murmured musically through the room, forming a deep pool just below where we stood, or rather
clung to the rope, for the incline at this point was
almost perpendicular. We enjoyed the scene far better,
no doubt, by virtue of the precarious footing from
which we viewed it. The fact that the conservatory
was inaccessible also lent enchantment to the view.
We could devise no means by which we could possibly
hope to reach the unattainable in this case, and as
each scheme proved futile, the beauties of the place
were enhanced. It seemed we should never tire of it.
For over an hour we gazed at the novel sights that
lay before us. In moving about to get different views
of the various objects we were straining on the rope
and see-sawing it on the edge of the rock where the
passage deflected from the perpendicular. Suddenly
the rope broke and the unattainable was ours before
you could say "Jack Robinson." Heels over head,
and repeat, we tumbled into the pool, which, fortunately, was deep enough to prevent us from receiving any bad bruises. It was a cold bath, and we
forgot all about the seriousness of the mishap in

wringing out our clothes and getting up a circulation.
We laughed and danced and yelled, carrying our
boisterousness to a pitch that must have astonished
the gods, if any of them were strolling through the
conservatory at that time. It was an hour after our
plunge into the "Tourists' Bath" before we began to
realize the situation, and it was just this: We should
probably starve to death in that dismal cave. Possibly the hunter might miss us in a day or two and
come to the rescue. Should the bear get the best of
him in their "tuss'l," even this hope must perish.
Succor from this source was a "bear" possibility indeed. Other tourists might visit the cave, but that
was a chance that we dared not depend on. It was
just possible that we might find another outlet. The
currents of air which we felt from time to time led us
to believe that there must be another opening to the
cavern. As near as we could determine, these air currents came from the direction from which the stream
flowed. Securing our rope, and the torches, which had
been used as staffs in making the first stage of our
descent, we started on a journey of exploration up
the stream. This latter was about eight feet wide and
two feet deep, and we frequently took deep draughts
of the water, not so much that we were thirsty, but
that its coolness, purity and sweetness made it a most
delicious beverage. For two miles, perhaps, we
journeyed along through a great variety of weird
and grotesque forms still lit up by the peculiar light
from overhead. Then the stream branched off from
the main cavern, coming now through a narrow

ravine, where we should have to wade in the water to longer guide our course by it. There were unmistakable indications, however, that the original bed of the stream was up the main hall, and we felt confident that by keeping up the old bed we should again come to the brook, where, in seeking a more direct route through the cavern, it had eaten its way through a softer formation. Again taking long draughts of the delicious water, we resumed our way up the great hall.

At two different places, probably two miles apart, the stream had widened to twelve or fifteen feet over shelving rocks, and must have formed beautiful cascades. After passing the second of these we paused to rest. Presently we caught the faint sound of a musical note. We held our breaths and listened; again and again we heard it—a far-away, deep, rich tone. We hurriedly pressed forward, the noise we made drowning out all other sounds. For ten minutes we trudged along and then stopped again to listen. We heard the same tones or notes, but there had been added others of still clearer and sweeter timbre. We pursued our way now with the least noise possible, fearful that we should lose one tone of the soft cadences which fell upon our eager ears. As we advanced, the tones multiplied, and the harmony grew in volume and sweetness, now low and plaintive, seeming to sweep the soul with every phase of human doubt and mystery and sorrow; then swelling out to full, joyous strains that spoke of rest and peace and triumph. We were in doubt as to whether we should proceed any farther. Surely we were intruding on some celestial choir. No human mind could have composed, or human hands executed, that sublime commingling of ecstatic sounds. It was like an æolian harp, of which the strings were chimes of bells, organ chords and vocal melodies vibrating to the touch of angels' wings. Believing, however, that natural causes must be at the bottom of this splendid music, we pressed forward, trembling with awe and delight. Finally we came upon the wonderful orchestra. Below us was a vast chamber, of which the hall in which we stood formed a sort of gallery. Myriads of stalactites hung from the roof, and as many stalagmites reared themselves from the slanting, uneven floor which formed the bed of a rushing cascade. Just beyond us the water had broken through the soft limestone bank and poured, in a broad thin sheet, into the room below, forming a beautiful waterfall. In its descent it touched innumerable stalactites, and reaching the floor it dashed in and out among a multitude of stalagmites. Any of these—stalactites or stalagmites—tapped with a lead pencil would give out a rich musical note; played upon by the water nymphs, the grand harmony which reverberated throughout the cavern was the result. The delicate resonant pendants from the roof vibrated in sympathy with the singing stalagmites below, and so played an undertone accompaniment to the leading pieces. Every swirl, swash, gurgle, splash, murmur and ripple of the waters found a melodious expression in the vibrations of some of

6

those glistening crystalline tubes. Not a sound of falling water or rushing torrent was to be heard. The roaring of a great cataract was all transformed into sweetest melody. As we stood listening, I was vividly reminded of some words of Cardinal Newman on music. "Is it possible," he says, "that that inexhaustible evolution and disposition of notes, so rich yet so simple, so intricate yet so regulated, so various yet so majestic, should be a mere sound which is gone and perishes? Can it be that those mysterious stirrings of heart, and keen emotions, and strange yearnings after we know not what, and awful impressions from we know not whence, should be wrought in us by what is unsubstantial, and comes and goes, and begins and ends in itself? It is not so; it cannot be. No; they have escaped from some higher sphere; they are the outpourings of eternal harmony in the medium of created sound; they are echoes from our Home; they are the voice of angels, or the Magnificat of saints, or the living laws of Divine Governance, or the Divine Attributes; something are they besides themselves, which we cannot compass, which we cannot utter—though mortal man, and he perhaps not otherwise distinguished above his fellows, has the gift of eliciting them."

The thrilling strains, which held us spell-bound, were indeed a divine symphony—a fitting prelude to the revelations of the next twenty-four hours.

Though our fatigue was forgotten under the charm of the music, we rested here for two hours. We had been traveling for ten hours, most of the time on smooth ground, and with good light all the time. It was rather curious that the light seemed to glow softer and yet brighter under the spell of the music, an effect, no doubt, of the sympathy of sight with hearing, but there had been no time when we could not see distinctly. The grade up which we had come we judged was about two hundred feet to the mile, and traveling at the rate of three miles an hour we calculated that we had reached an altitude of six thousand feet above the point from which we started, and hence must be near the summit of some lofty mountain.

After our rest we marched on to the inspiring strains of the water orchestra, feeling as greatly refreshed as if we had enjoyed a good sleep and partaken of food. We had not proceeded far when we noticed that the air currents were cooler and stronger, blowing steadily in our faces. The peculiar light also began to fade out in the stronger light of day. Following the stream, which had once more become our guide, around a slight curve, we saw, not far ahead, the opening for which we had been looking, and through which was pouring the first rays of the morning sun. The stream also came through the opening, there being a space above the water about three feet high and six feet wide. Through this opening we looked out upon a small lake, fed, undoubtedly, from below, as it lay almost on the summit of a lofty mountain. It was about fifty yards across the lake to a point where the sloping bank would allow us to climb out. This point was directly ahead of us, and us the sunbeams came from a point considerably to the right, we must have been looking due north. The water, contracted to a much narrower bed, flowed from the lake in a strong current about four feet deep. We should be compelled to force our way against this for only about six feet, and making our clothes up into compact bundles, which we tied on our heads, we made our way through the channel, and struck out boldly for the opposite shore. The water seemed to be only a degree or two above the freezing point, and our swim was anything but sport. Our clothes, however, were dry, and we were again comfortable by the time we were dressed. Climbing the little slope, we found ourselves on a perfectly level table-land, containing, probably, two acres, and forming the apex of the mountain. The first object that attracted our attention was an unusually large piano box, as we took it to be, situated in the center of the plateau. On closer examination it proved to be fastened to a heavy floor or platform, with large iron hinges on one side and a common hasp and staple on the opposite side. It was not locked, and though a little afraid of some mammoth Jack-in-the-box trick, we raised the box, disclosing an instrument of delicate and complicated parts. It showed fine workmanship, and seemed to combine telegraphic and telephonic apparatus. One of the students, who was an expert telegrapher, expressed the opinion that it had been built with a view to transmitting messages on some principle of ethereal vibrations. Mel regarded it as an instrument to be used in conveying to a deaf audience

the words of the lecturer addressing it. Jim thought
"that if it were a contrivance for catching and frying
fish we couldn't get it to working any too soon to suit
him." This reminded us that we were hungry. We
could still catch a few notes of the orchestra, but the
nervous energy imparted by its inspiriting tones had
died out, leaving us tired, sleepy and hungry.

We now took a view of our surroundings. As far
north as we could see the mountains continued, veering
a little to the west, while here and there isolated peaks
or spurs, covered with tall pine trees, jutted out from
the principal chain into the open country to the east
of us. To the west and south it was all mountains.
On the west side of the plateau which we occupied, we
found a trail leading down the mountain. Following
this trail for a mile we came to a beautiful valley, and
what was more to the purpose, a large, comfortable
looking log house. Three white men and an old negro
were busy loading a wagon with the various parts of
an instrument similar to the one we had just seen on
the mountain. The men referred us to their employer,
who was in the house, assuring us that he would see
that our wants were provided for. We proceeded to
the house and knocked at the door, which was opened
by an old gentleman with long, silvery hair and
beard. We told our story briefly, and asked for food
and shelter until the following day, when we should
be sufficiently refreshed to make the journey back to
camp. We were cordially welcomed, and the colored
man, who answered to the call "Pete," was soon preparing our breakfast with the skill and celerity of

an experienced cook. Very agreeably to us we were shortly invited to "set up an' help yo'selves." While we were eating the old gentleman told us his story.

His name was Gaston Lesage, and he was a Frenchman by birth and education. At the age of thirty he came to this country and became, as he frankly confessed, a monomaniac on the subjects of electricity and telegraphy, his pet hobby being to invent and perfect an instrument for the transmission of soundsigns by natural electrical currents. He had had an ample fortune, and had spared neither pains nor expense in the endeavor to put his theories into practice. The only encouragement received had been in the fourth year of his experiments, when he had succeeded in establishing communications between the two instruments which his ingenuity had devised, but at very short range and only under certain favorable conditions of the atmosphere. He had carried on his researches and experiments on land and at sea, in the burning desert and on lonely islands, and was now closing a series of experiments covering a period of three years on these lofty mountain peaks. He was still unsuccessful, and was that day packing up one of his instruments preparatory to abandoning the enterprise altogether. The next day he intended to pack up the remaining instrument, which would have to be taken to pieces and carried down to the house on *burros.* He and his men had been six months in constructing the rough road that had enabled them to reach the valley they now occupied. It would take us about two days to make the trip down the mountain over this road. Our late breakfast dispatched, we betook ourselves to sleep, having first exacted a promise from Mr. Lesage to call us for the evening meal.

It was near sundown when we were aroused by heavy thunder, and got up to find it raining, or misting, as we appeared to be in the cloud itself. With some alarm we remembered now that we had not closed the case of the instrument, and expressed the fear to Mr. Lesage that it would be damaged by the rain. He assured us that it would sustain no injury from a fog like the one driving along the mountains, even if it reached the summit, which he doubted. After supper our host volunteered to take us to the summit and explain the mechanism of the instruments from the one yet in working order. We gladly accepted the offer, though it was now a little after dark. Having first lit a lantern of extraordinary power, the old gentleman led the way up the steep trail. The lantern, however, was carried by Pete, the sable cook, who brought up the rear. At first the light threw our gigantic shadows on the surrounding mist, then we passed beyond the cloud to find the stars shining brightly overhead. The temperature had fallen several degrees, and a light wind was blowing from the south. Arriving at the summit, we found a magnificent view awaiting us. The open land to the north, east and south, as far as we could see, was filled with a mass of great billowy clouds illuminated with a deep flush by the incessant play of sheet lightning. It was as if we stood on the shore of a great, rosy sea stretching far away to wonderland. As we

looked we perceived far to the north the first tremu-
lous streamers of the *aurora borealis.* At the sight
of this, Mr. Lesage became greatly excited, and his
laments and self-blaming for having taken to pieces
his other instrument, which would require days to
put together again, were painful to hear. "The appearance of the northern lights," he said, "at this
time of the year, indicates a very unusual electrical
condition of the solar system." With that certainty
born of the inability of verification, he felt sure that
had his other instrument been in position, he would at
last have discovered the true nature of the electrical
currents.

Higher and higher streamed the crimson banners
of the north, irradiating the heavens with glory and
effulgence. The billowy mist threw back the roseate
splendor, and in the growing light the isolated peaks
were seen here and there lifting their crowns of tall
trees above the glowing waves like great masts and
spars of ocean craft—great vessels, seeming in the
universal glow to be carved from radiant coral. The
rising wind, coming directly from the cavern, bore to
our ears the full, joyous peals of the orchestra. The
clouds began to move away to the north, and, as they
swept by the peaks, the latter sailed toward us—
splendid ships coming to bear us over that mystic sea
to the regions of glorious light where the mysteries of
existence should be revealed, where all doubts should
be swept away and the "strange yearnings" after the
Infinite be satisfied.

"Tick, tick-tick, tickety-tick," suddenly chattered

the instrument. "Mon Dieu!" exclaimed the old gentleman, reverting to the mother tongue in his excitement.

"Click-click, click, clickety-clickety click," again from the instrument. Our host's face grew ghastly in the red light. He threw his hands over his heart, trembling and gasping for breath. The negro was supporting his employer, though his own teeth were chattering like castanets. "Fo' de Lawd's sake, Marse Gaston," he yelled in his fright, "smash de deb'lish ting an' frow um in de lake."

After the second "call" there had come a perfect torrent of clicks and ticks, continued for a minute or so with such rapidity and force that it seemed the instrument must be lifted off its base. Then, as if the mysterious operator was satisfied with this exhibition of his dexterity, the clickings assumed a slower pace. By this time Mr. Lesage had recovered himself and was giving his whole attention to the instrument. The Auroraphone we there and then named it. Pete's teeth were less noisy, but his eyes were still protruding, as he stood looking askance at "de deb'lish ting," his body leaning slightly toward the home trail, all ready to cut and run at the first sign of danger.

The telegrapher of our party was now with Mr. Lesage, listening to the clickings, which were unintelligible to both. The breeze freshened, bringing in clearer tones the thrilling cadences of the orchestra. The skies flamed out brighter and brighter, the clouds rolled along faster and faster, and the stately ships sailed toward port with increasing speed. The auroraphone clicked away first after one regular system, and then after another, pausing a minute or so between them. During one of these intervals the student, on a sudden impulse, put his hand to the key and dashed off in the Morse alphabet, "Who are you, what are you, and where are you?" The auroraphone clicked away as before for several minutes, then ceased altogether. At the end of ten minutes there came in the Morse alphabet these answers to the questions asked: "I am Rulph Bozar. I am a human being much like yourselves, and I am an inhabitant of the ringed planet, sixth in order from the sun,"—Saturn, as Mr. Lesage, who adhered to the former pronunciation, informed us. "By the natural electrical currents," continued the auroraphone, "I am enabled to send and receive messages to and from various planets, and with a velocity far exceeding the rate at which light travels. By means of an instrument which we call the optigraph, attached to our plano-electrophone, I am also enabled to see you and your party, nine of you. Tell our colored brother, who, I see, is momentarily expecting an explosion, that there is no cause for alarm. Please tell me the names by which you designate both your own and our planet, so that in speaking of them I may use the terms with which you are familiar."

The information was forwarded, and we must wait ten minutes for a response. In the meantime Mr. Lesage endeavored to allay Pete's fears. He assured him that there was no danger and told him that by a wonderful chance we had "established communication with Saturn—" But here Pete's teeth began to chatter again and he broke out: "I done tole yo' so, I did. I know'd it wa' ole Satan, and fo' de lub ob de Lawd, Marse Gaston, quit foolin' wid de ole debil an' come home wid Pete," and he led the way down the mountain with none to follow, at a pace that soon took him out of sight and hearing.

Again the auroraphone is clicking:

"My Brethren of the Earth, Greeting:

"You will first want to know how it is that I understand your language and system of telegraphy. With us both are obsolete, and were in use just five hundred years ago, which, as you measure time, would be fifteen thousand years ago. I hold a position in what we term an electro-planetary station, and to fill the position I must be somewhat acquainted with the rudiments of many old languages and systems of telegraphy, and among those I have studied are your own. Please bear in mind that I have to divide my attention among a great many of these old languages; that the one I am now using has long been out of date, and hence you must not be surprised that I am far less proficient in it than your own men of letters. The age in which your language was used by our nation is known as the Solarian age. We called the central orb of the solar system the Sun, which was regarded as the creator of the universe—as God. The Solarian era dates from the advent of a wonderful and good man who established a great religion. He claimed that he came from the Sun, and was the son of God— the Sun; that he was one with the Sun—was God. Although this religion has long been discarded as containing many superstitions, now no longer necessary, yet all reverence is accorded it by our people, who are at one in attributing to it our present culture and progress. We have a new era now, dating from the advent of a new religion, which 'Unitarianism' comes nearest defining in your language—meaning not so much the unity of God, or of mankind, as the one-hood of the universe. As before said, we are in communication with several other planets, which we have reached by means of our electro-planetary stations, where operators are employed to keep a constant look-out for a favorable chance to introduce ourselves to neighboring worlds. At certain stages of progress, the people of the various planets carry their inventiveness to the production of instruments like your own, and sooner or later we reach them. Owing to the unusual electrical disturbance of the past hour, I have had a view of the earth's entire surface, and hence was enabled to adjust the plano-electrophone so as to be in direct communication with your instrument. Now that we know your exact location we shall have no further trouble in communicating with each other, and by adding a power or two of artificial electricity I can see you by the same currents that I use in sending messages. There will be times when, for a day, or even for a week, conditions will be unfavorable for an exchange of messages. Our electrometer, however, warns us of all electrical changes, so that we can tell for weeks ahead when conditions will be favorable and unfavorable. For thirty-six hours yet, as you measure time, we may communicate, and then

for three days unfavorable conditions will prevail.
Our inventors are at work on some new processes for
generating electricity, which promise much. With
them we shall be independent of natural electrical
currents.

"In giving you a history of our religious, social
and political institutions, I shall begin with the
former, and, indeed, I shall devote myself to that
mainly, and treat of the others incidentally. Our
present religion or philosophy is based on the results
of certological calculations. Certology is with us a
science which is to logic as your geometry is to guess-
work. Our knowledge of the universe, obtained through
certology, is such that among the eighteen hundred
millions of our people there is perfect unanimity as to
its origin, purpose and destiny. For want of terms
I cannot give you an insight into the principles and
methods of this modern science, but the earlier history
of our progress can be set forth in terms with which
you are familiar.

"The religion of the son of the Sun taught the immortality of the soul, future rewards for right-doing
and future punishment for wrong-doing. Creeto was
the prophet's name who revealed this religion, and we
are still known as Creetans and so I shall call our people when speaking of them. Another great nation to
the west of us also had their inspired prophet, or
teacher, who taught the existence of an invisible
spiritual God, who would eventually absorb all mortal souls after they had served as the souls of other
beings and persons — 'transmigration of souls,' they

call it. There were also skeptics, who denied and ridiculed both religions, claiming that the universe was self-existent, and that neither the Sun nor the spiritual God was its creator. They moreover contended that death was the extinction of the conscious soul. Many other religions and philosophies were extant, but teaching only different phases of these three.

"In the course of time a great mathematician, Lapassa, brought out the Solar theory, and I shall quote from a later writer a brief presentation of its general features.

"'The first cosmological speculation,' says Johann Feske, 'which has been raised quite above the plane of guess-work by making no other assumption than that of the uniformity of nature, is the well-known Solar theory. Every astronomer knows that Sexbellus, like all other cosmical bodies which are flattened at the poles, was formerly a mass of fluid, and consequently filled a much larger space than at present. It is further agreed on all hands that the Sun is a contracting body, since there is no other possible way of accounting for the enormous quantity of heat which he generates. The so-called primeval nebula follows as a necessary inference from these facts. There was once a time when Sexbellus was distended on all sides away out to the Trios* and beyond it, so that the matter now contained in the Trios was then a part of our equatorial zone. And at a still remoter date in the past the mass of the Sun was diffused in

---

* The third, or outermost, ring of Saturn.

every direction beyond the orbit of Octo,* and no planet had an individual existence, for all were indistinguishable parts of the solar mass. When the great mass of the Sun, increased by the relatively small mass of all the planets put together, was spread out in this way, it was a rare vapor or gas. At the period where the question is taken up in Lapassa's treatment of the Solar theory, the shape of this mass is regarded as spheroidal; but at an earlier period its shape may well have been as irregular as that of any of the nebulæ which we now see in distant parts of the heavens, for, whatever its primitive shape, the equalization of its rotation would in time make it spheroidal.

"'That the quantity of rotation was the same then as now is unquestionable; for no system, great or small, can acquire or lose rotation by any action going on within itself, any more than a man could pick himself up by the waist band and lift himself over a wall. So that the primitive rotating spheroidal solar nebula is not a matter of assumption, but is just what must once have existed, provided there has been no breach of continuity in nature's operations. Now proceeding to reason back from the past to the present, it has been shown that the abandonment of successive equatorial belts by the contracting solar mass must have ensued in accordance with known mechanical laws; and in similar wise, under ordinary circumstances, each belt must have parted into frag-

* Neptune.

ments and the fragments chasing each other around
the same orbit must have at last coalesced into a
spheroidal planet. Not only this, but it has also
been shown that as the result of such a process the
relative sizes of the planets would be likely to take
the order which they now follow; that the ring immediately succeeding that of Golath* would be likely
to abort and produce a great number of tiny planets
instead of one good-sized one; that the outer planets
would be likely to have many moons, and that Sexbellus,† besides having the greatest number of moons,
would be likely to retain some of his inner rings un-
broken; that Opak‡ would be likely to have a long
day and Golath a short one; that the extreme outer
planets would be not unlikely to rotate in a retro-
grade direction; and so on through a long list of interesting and striking details. Not only, therefore,
are we driven to the inference that our solar system
was once a vaporous nebula, but we find that the
mere contraction of such a nebula, under the influence
of the enormous mutual gravitation of its particles,
carries with it the explanation of both the more general and the more particular features of the present
system, so that we may fairly regard this stupendous
process as veritable matter of history.,

---

* Jupiter.
† Saturn.
‡ The earth. Mr. Bozar quoted the exact language of
the book, neglecting to use the names by which we designated the planets, but afterwards gave us their equivalents,
as just shown.

"In confirmation of this theory—that everything is from the Sun, which originally existed in a nebulous mass, it was discovered that there were other nebulous masses throughout the universe, in a gaseous state, and undergoing concentration. I quote from another writer on this subject. Sir Wilhelm Drooper, in speaking of the difficulty of determining the condition of remote nebula by means of the telescope, says: 'Fortunately, however, other means for the settlement of this question are available. A few years ago, it was discovered that the spectrum of an ignited solid is continuous—that is, has neither dark nor bright lines. Others had previously made known that the spectrum of ignited gases is discontinuous. Here, then, is the means of determining whether the light emitted by a given nebula comes from an incandescent gas or from a congeries of solids, stars or suns. If its spectrum be discontinuous, it is a true nebula or gas; if continuous, a congeries of stars.

"'Subsequent observations have shown that, of sixty nebulæ examined, nineteen give discontinuous or gaseous spectra; the remainder, continuous ones.

"'It may, therefore, be admitted that physical evidence has at length been obtained demonstrating the existence of vast masses of matter in a gaseous condition and at a temperature of incandescence. The hypothesis of Lapassa has thus a firm basis. In such a nebular mass, cooling by radiation is a necessary incident, and condensation and rotation the inevitable results. There must be a separation of rings, all lying in one plane, a generation of planets and

7

satellites all rotating alike—a central sun and engirdling globes. From a chaotic mass, through the
operation of natural laws, an organized system has
been produced. An integration of matter into worlds
has taken place through a decline of heat.'

"I might quote from other of our scientists on this
subject, but, to be brief, I may say that the evidence
became so conclusive that the Solar theory was universally accepted by our nation. Then the philosophers pointed to the fact that the teachings of
Creeto in some respects were true. The Sun was the
creator or parent of our planet, and imparted to it
all its life, animal and vegetable, just as Creeto had
taught, and hence he, Creeto, himself was the son of
the Sun, in a sense. It was further prophesied, that as
Creeto's teachings had been so productive of good,
thus showing their harmony with progress, further knowledge of the universe would prove him
right in other respects. His had been a great moral
system, and accordingly his principles must have
been consistent with truth. The next question that
came up for adjustment was the doctrine of immortality. According to the Solar theory man is the
outcome of development—the result of the same natural forces that have produced our planet. Now, it
follows from the origin of the planets, that in the
course of time they must cool down and return to the
parent mass, the Sun; and the planets and Sun thus
colliding must reduce the whole mass to a nebulous
condition, to again undergo the process of world-
making. The planets must necessarily be reproduced,

and man, as being an inseparable part of the planets, must also be reproduced. But as each solar nebula must lose some of its energy through the radiation of heat, it was evident that it could not be exactly the same planets or men that would come into being at each successive evolution of the solar nebula. But what becomes of the heat, or radiant energy?

"Before taking up this question, I suppose you will want to partake of the refreshments which I see our colored friend is bringing you, and as it is my own lunch time we shall rest for a while."

Just then we heard Pete's voice from some point down the trail: "Spoze yo' all can't quit talkin' wid dat ole debil long 'nuff to come an' git er cup er hot coffee?" It was evident that the cook was not going to come any nearer. We were somewhat chilled, and hungry as a matter of course, and the unmistakable odor of hot coffee in the air made us feel very kindly disposed towards our colored friend. If the refreshments would not come to us we should go to the refreshments. Mr. Lesage and the student retained their positions at the auroraphone, as if fearful to lose sight of it for an instant, while the rest of us hurried down to Pete.

"Ain't Marse Gaston comin'?" he asked. We answered in the negative, and hastened to assure him that we would carry the provision up to Mr. Lesage, and eat it there.

"No, yo' ain't gwine to do nuffen ob de kind. None ob dese vittles gwine onto unconsecrated groun' ef ole Pete knows hisse'f," and he tightened his grip on the handles of a monster steaming coffee-pot and a huge basket. "Ef yo' all promis' not to take nuffen to Marse Gaston yo' can help yo'selves." We immediately promised, and Mel went back to tell Mr. Lesage and the student that they would have to come to Pete if they wanted lunch. He returned in a few moments accompanied by the others. While we were regaling ourselves on the hot, fragrant coffee and delicious sandwiches, Mr. Lesage again essayed to put Pete right in regard to the discovery we had made. "We were not sending messages to the devil," he said, addressing Pete, "but to Saturn, the planet——"

"Oh course Satan planned it," vociferated Pete. "Dat's ole Belzebub eb'ry time. Same ole debil been lay'n snar's and plan'en to get de Lawd's chil'un eb'ry since de world's been made." It was impossible for Mr. Lesage or any of the rest of us to convince him that we were not in league with his Satanic majesty, and but for the final culmination of the matter, powerful and terrific as it was, he would, perhaps, have retained his wrong idea.

Pete's thoughtfulness for our welfare, however, was partly a scheme to prevail upon his employer not to sell himself to Satan. He had thought that if he could get Mr. Lesage beyond the immediate influence of the evil one, he could persuade him not to return, and he now fell to begging and entreating him to go home, in a way that made us pity him, for it all grew out of his deep concern and love for his employer. Mr. Lesage was very gentle and patient with his old companion, for such he was, rather than a mere serv-

ing-man. Pete had been his most faithful attendant
for thirty years, the old gentleman paying him nomi-
nal wages and providing for his every want and need.
A few days after Mr. Lesage's arrival in this country
his life had been saved by Pete. Mr. Lesage was driving a fractious team, which, having become frightened
and unmanageable, must have hurled themselves and
driver over a high embankment but for Pete's
timely interference. Mr. Lesage had made inquiries
about the brave negro, found him a slave, bought
him, made him free, and took him into his own employ. Pete could neither read nor write, but it was
his boast that without knowing a letter he had
learned telegraphy, and, within the limits of his mea-
gre vocabulary, he had learned it. With his acute
sense of hearing and powers of imitation, he had
learned by entire words to send and receive simple
messages, and he had been Mr. Lesage's most valuable assistant in his experiments. Pete's knowledge
of telegraphy and the instruments was such that the
ticking of the instrument without any apparent cause
led him to refer it to the supernatural, and occurring
under such weird circumstances, and mistaking his
employer's agitation for fright, he had attributed the
whole matter to an evil rather than to a beneficent
spirit. The idea once fixed in his mind that we were
in communication with the evil one, everything was
thereafter construed into a confirmation of his
error. It was with genuine dismay and grief that he
watched his employer hurry back to the auroraphone.
Some of us lingered behind and helped Pete gather up

the tin cups and platters used during the meal. Just
before he started down the trail Pete went a little
aside and picked up a big heavy overcoat and asked
us to take it to "Marse Gaston." The old gentleman
was very glad to ensconce himself in the warm, heavy
folds of the great coat. For the first time we now
thought of building a fire. There was a quantity of
dry quaking asp poles near at hand and we soon had
a great pile of them blazing and crackling in a comfortable manner. The clouds had by this time nearly
disappeared, and the quivering light of the skies had
almost faded out. When the first intelligible message
had been received, Mr. Lesage had taken from a
drawer in the instrument some blocks of paper, and
he and the student had written down messages simultaneously, so far as recorded.

Our Saturnian friend seemed to require considerable time for lunch, and the student finally "called"
Saturn. In ten minutes' time came the answering
clicks: "I returned from lunch quite awhile ago, but
picked up the 'Hourly News' which had been brought
in, and became interested in an article on 'The Military Game,' of which more anon. It was right to call
me, so long as it was done respectfully. I may as well
warn you now that anything like disrespect, impa-
tience or presumption will not be permitted. Only
yesterday two planets were debarred from further
communication with us, and severely censured for im-
pertinence; and our displeasure, I assure you, is expressed in a very sudden and impressive manner.
You will wonder at the necessity of such severity on

the part of a highly developed and benevolent people; but it is vitally necessary for reasons which you cannot now understand.

"We were speaking of the disposition of the heat, or radiant energy of the universe. A result of the constant radiation of heat was evident—the entire solar system must at length be reduced to a dead, black, frozen mass. But if this were a possible result, why had it not already been consummated, as there had been infinite past time for its completion? Because, the scientists answered, our system is but a tiny part of another greater system, and when in the past its energy became expended, it has collided with the other members of the greater system, and so has again and again been restored to life and activity. This, however, was only to postpone the final death of our system, for sooner or later this greater system must itself radiate away all its energy and become motionless and dead. At this point many claimed that we should have to accept the spiritual deity over and above the universe of our neighboring nation, to sustain our system, or else look forward to its final death; and even in this case be unable to account for the fact that it was not already dead. But our scientists saw no reason why they should stop short of making this last greater system a part of one great system including the whole cosmos, and hence its life be sustained indefinitely. Indefinitely, but not infinitely, for the cosmos as a whole must run its course and end with all its energy dissipated in the form of radiant heat. Our scientists did not commit the error of contending that the condensation of worlds into greater and greater systems could go on to infinity at the expense of an infinite number of worlds, scattered throughout infinite space. To make our system a part of the one great system was to establish our kinship with the entire cosmos; our union with any other system by gravitation depended on that kinship, and that kinship depended on the fact that we had at one time been a part of the mass toward which we were gravitating. Hence we could not go on forever traveling back to a point from which we must have at one time started. We must finally get back to the one original mass, to be again thrown out into systems of minor worlds. This original mass, it was evident, must be isolated from any other great system of worlds, that might possibly be looked to for a new supply of energy, imparted by colliding with it; to suppose such other system of worlds was to assume that it was only a part of our own system, or our system a part of it, if by any law we were to renew our life by colliding with it, and hence we must consider the two as forming the one original mass, and so considered, there was nothing now to prevent the complete radiation of energy and final death. The scientists now maintained that the question need not and should not be pushed so far, not that they cared for the ultimate doom of the universe, but that they could not explain, from the principles on which the Solar theory was itself based, why this final doom had not already overtaken us. It was the wise men of the nation to the west of us that persisted in pushing these cosmological questions so far. A few years prior to the time the subject had reached the above phase, their teachers had tried to prove to our scholars the existence of the spiritual deity they worshiped, by an argument founded on causation. Everything, they maintained, is caused or determined by some preceding event, and this event is caused by some prior event, and so on backward in the chain of cause and effect until we must come to the First Cause. But our scholars had asked, if everything is caused, who or what created the First Cause, or caused God? They had replied, reasonably enough, that the question must not be pushed to such an extent. But our scholars scoffed at them greatly, for being afraid to accept the consequences of their own logic. And now our scientists, to their shame, stood up and unblushingly asked their former opponents not to push the question so far, on the plea that when carried so far beyond the possibility of verification it became mere speculation, both unprofitable and unmanageable, as if a single inference in the whole theory of solar evolution could at that time be verified. They were not long, however, in realizing that if the higher application of their physical principles was mere speculation, so it had been all along the line of argument. If a comparatively small mass of matter like the Sun would cool down by radiation, so must the mass, so inconceivably greater, formed of all the planets and suns cool down by radiation. And if this refrigeration was to take place in the comparatively short time they predicted, they

could but feel under obligations to give some account
of what the universe had been doing in all past time.
If the tiny planet on which we lived was related to the
mass into which it must finally be precipitated, as
child to parent, so must the greatest system of which
we could conceive be related to any greater mass
with which it could possibly collide. These things
must be met boldly and overcome, or else in consistency the whole Solar theory must be abandoned.
From the fact that matter was making its way back
to a starting-point the conclusion was forced upon us
that the universe was limited. That our limited universe was not already dead forced upon us the conclusion that the surrounding ethereal medium, by which
heat is enabled to radiate away, is itself limited.
Thus the energy of the universe was preserved and its
eternal existence assured. It was undergoing a great
cycle, one half of which was evolution, the other half
dissolution. It had been undergoing this process
throughout all past time and would so continue
throughout all future time, each cycle being followed
by another, exactly like the preceding one. The limitation and eternal activity of the universe are now
demonstrated with simple accuracy under theorem
first of Certology. I see through the optigraph that
you are looking out into starry space with renewed
interest.

"Our optigraph we regard as our most wonderful
invention, as it enables us to see much that is going
on in our neighboring planets, but only in the larger
cities, or where we are connected with an instrument

like yours and employing several powers of artificial electricity for the purpose of seeing. The jar of machinery, the roar of traffic, the vibrations of heat which ascend from your commercial centres form an electrical current with which we connect a current from our optigraph—a natural current in this case—and the whole city and immediate surroundings become visible. Nothing is hid from our view, clouds, walls, and the earth itself, becoming transparent with this subtile electrical medium. We cannot exactly read mind, but from the play of the features we can determine your people's inmost thoughts. I could anticipate your wishes and determine your intentions, by running the optigraph all the time, but the expense is so great that this is not permissible. With the cities it is different, and at all times their secrets are open to us. Oh, the deeds of crime and wrong which we daily see going on! Later you will understand with what grief we behold these sad things—sad, for we know how everything gained by oppression and injustice must be atoned for, not only by the oppressor but by all of human kind. You will wonder why we view these things if they are painful to us, and we are powerless to prevent them. True, we are powerless to a certain extent, but the knowledge that we behold their acts can but have a wholesome effect on the morals of the people resident in your great cities.

"In tracing the Solar theory to limitation, I omitted many particulars. At one point the religionists protested against the theory on the ground that it had a tendency to destroy the common belief in the special creations of the Sun-god. But when it was understood that the Sun was the source of the energy by which all phenomena were created, it only increased their reverence for their Sun-god to learn the process of evolution by which he worked. The life and material of our bodies being thus referred to the Supreme Being did much toward satisfying the religious sentiment. But more difficulty was experienced when the people were called upon to give up their belief that the Sun was the true god. Science had shown that there was a more remote sun or central orb to which we owed allegiance and on which we depended for existence. But the Sun could be seen, its warmth was felt, and its beneficent influence was everywhere apparent. To give up this deity for one not so readily perceived, even though this more remote one was grander, more complex and powerful, was hard to do. But the truth triumphed and the greater deity was generally accepted.

"The atheists now came to the front with the assertion that this was rank polytheism, which was equivalent to no god at all. Their argument was that we first had a Sun-god, then another greater god to which the first paid homage, and then a still more remote god on which the first two depended, and so on. As there was no absolute central orb, consequently there was no true god. It was not until science had demonstrated the limitation of the universe, and that consequently there was an absolute center, that the religionists and atheists met on the common ground that there was one true god, and that was the universe as a whole. There was unanimity among all classes on that point, and also that the first duty of intelligent beings was to learn the order of manifestation of this Universe-god.

"Man was now regarded as a group of particles or atoms, peculiarly combined, each particle endowed with its portion of the divine force that moved and sustained the universe. Then there must come a time when each individual man must be reproduced—must live again, just as he is now living. God could not die, he must ever continue active. His substance was limited, and consequently there must come a time when every possible new combination of these limited particles must be exhausted—when no new combinations can be effected even by deity himself. Then the combination which now exists, and of which we are a part, must be reproduced, and we ourselves along with it. Thus we are immortal. Sooner or later we must in the very nature of things live again. Never can we disappear from the scene.

"With the nation's acceptance of the doctrine of immortality there was a decided improvement in its morals. Wrong-doing, it was known, resulted in suffering, and right-doing, as a general thing, resulted in a gain of pleasure, both to the right-doer and to the community. With the realization that the painful results of evil deeds were for all eternity, and that the happy results of good deeds were also eternal, much stronger motives for right-doing were everywhere presented. Science had again attested to

the soundness of Creeto's teachings, in this declaration
of future rewards and punishments for deeds done in
this life. The proofs of the doctrine of immortality
and its ethical bearings are now found under theorem
second of Certology.

"The most important political result of the new
moral life was the abolition of slavery. Up to that
time slavery had been considered a necessary condition to social stability. It was an institution under
which many forms of suffering, injustice and ignorance were imposed upon a great class of human beings, but was tolerated on the plea that we could not
get along without it. But when men began to realize
that the wrongs growing out of slavery must always
be repeated—in other words, were eternal wrongs,—a
great effort was made to abolish the evil, and at the
expense of a bloody war the slaves were freed. This
was a great advance, and for many years our people
enjoyed a peace and prosperity that compensated for
the many hard-fought battles in the cause of human
liberty. Then the power of wealth began to be felt,
and the result was that it soon enslaved a greater
number of our citizens than there had been serfs in
the days of slavery's greatest power. And now the
yoke was laid upon the very bone and sinew of the
nation's life. Disturbances, riots and civil wars grew
out of this condition of affairs. The monopolies and
wealthy classes, however, always triumphed. Deeper
wrongs and greater oppressions were more common
than when men were made slaves by law. These
wrongs were also recognized as eternal, but the greed

for money seemed to have deafened all classes to the cries of humanity and completely numbed the moral sense. The rich were in power. They were wise enough to sacrifice individual prejudices and opinions for the common good of their class, and gained by the spirit of unity that this disposition generated. Thus, while in the minority, they could so shape the government that their enterprises were all carried on lawfully, regardless of how oppressive their measures might be to the poorer classes. These latter were, as a general thing, more loyal to the government than their more fortunate masters, and prided themselves on their patriotism, which, of course, was just so much more capital to those whose financial interests were guarded by the government. The arrogance and complacency of the aristocrats made the poor only more envious, reckless, inefficient and miserable. By the use of our improved electrical guns the masses could wreak sudden and terrible vengeance for their many wrongs, when goaded to the point of riot and rebellion, but the reaction was far more terrible on them, and after suffering greater losses and hardships than they inflicted, they would be again cowed and become toiling millions for their masters.

"Labor-saving inventions, which should have been a boon to all, rather added to the poverty of the poor. Machinery had, in fact, been brought to such a perfection, that it seemed to be endowed with greater intelligence than many of the common laborers. By means of this machinery the nation's power of production was prodigious. The nation's aggregate wealth, however, would not have sufficed, if equally distributed, to have given more than a mere pittance to each family. But it was evident that if the nation's power of production was rightly directed and economized all would have an abundance. The economists formulated many remedies for the evil, presented pages and pages bristling with statistics, prophesied glorious times for the future, and accomplished nothing. Besides our civil strifes we were every few years at war with neighboring nations. You will bear in mind that our years equal about thirty of yours, and that our average of life is sixty of these long years. Our days, however, are about half as long as yours. Owing to our many moons and luminous rings our nights are similar to your cloudy days, and our cloudiest nights are as your brightest moonlight nights. I now see by the general activity of your cities that morning is at hand. You will want your usual meal and you need rest. No doubt you are willing to hear more of our history, but I must dismiss you for the day. To-night, if you wish, I shall be pleased to continue, but until then adieu."

In fact we were tired, and though deeply interested we were glad to rest. We went to the house, had breakfast, and then slept soundly until noon. After dinner, accompanied by our new friends, we visited the cave. We first made a pole raft, on which we pushed ourselves to a very good landing just within the cavern. We spent the afternoon enjoying the subterranean wonders. Our friends had often heard the music, but the strong current flowing into the dark, forbidding hole had made them afraid to investigate its cause. It was a source of pleasure to ourselves to witness their surprise and delight at each new scene presented to view, or at some deeper and richer cadence from the orchestra. We returned to "the retreat," as Mr. Lesage called his home, in time for an early supper, and as the shades of night began to fall we were again on the summit of the mountain, Mr. Lesage and the student stationed at the auroraphone, the rest of us lounging around the fire which we had built. Presently the anxiously expected clickings were heard and we were all attention. True, those of us who could not understand the sound-characters gained nothing by listening, but until the student passed us his pages, which he did from time to time, to be read among ourselves, we became as deeply absorbed in those mysterious clickings as the two operators themselves.

CHAPTER V.

THE DUMMIES' REVOLT.

"THE nation to the west of us," clicked the auroraphone, "was a great and warlike people, with whom we were often at war. They made it part of their religion to enforce their peculiar tenets and beliefs on other nations. These were the people I have before mentioned, as teaching the existence of an invisible, spiritual God, the transmigration of souls, and the final total oblivion of mankind by its absorption into the one great spirit. They had made great progress in the arts and sciences, but none in religion. Centuries before, their prophet, declaring himself to be the Son of God, had given them their religion, and they still adhered to its principles and precepts. They had also established their religion in other countries, civilized and heathen. Many of their wise men ranked higher in the scale of wisdom and goodness than our own teachers and philosophers. We should not have objected to their establishing their churches among our people, but we had observed that wherever their religion was introduced their national vice of intemperance was sure to follow—a vice practically unknown to our citizens. While a few of their wise men excelled our most gifted scholars and philanthropists, yet, owing to the evil of drunkenness, mill-

ions of their people were far lower than the worst of
ours. They called us heathen and gross materialists,
but our people were universally happier, and we were
content. During one of our civil wars, this nation invaded our frontier and gained possession of one of
our outlying provinces. When a few years later we
regained our territory, what was our grief to find
many of our countrymen raving maniacs, made so by
intemperance. At the time our troops entered the regained province, several of its citizens were in prison
for having killed their own children, some for having
murdered their wives, others for raising their hands
against their own parents. The news of this terrible
condition of affairs spread like wild-fire throughout
the country. There was a general uprising; all classes
were united and acted in unison; war was declared; vol-
unteers poured into the recruiting posts; armies were
equipped and put into the field, and departing from
our time-honored policy of acting only on the defensive,
we now assumed the offensive and invaded the enemies' territory. They fought well, stimulated to almost demoniacal onslaughts by their 'fighting whis-
key,' as they called it. But our troops were better
disciplined, more manageable, hardier and healthier;
our generals cooler-headed; officers and men were
stimulated by the memory of the terrible afflictions
brought upon their fellow-citizens, and they defeated
the enemy in almost every battle. In less than a year
their capital and principal cities were devastated and
they sued for peace on any terms. Our government
insisted on but two conditions: First, they must

pledge themselves on their nation's honor to make no further attempts to carry their religion into other countries until they had first freed their own from the curse of intemperance; second, they must pay liberal pensions to the families of which any member had become a victim to drink. The terms were accepted and the war ended.

"Our government now had time to deal with the plague of intemperance in its own province. Fifteen hundred inebriates were enrolled on the pension list. One thousand of these were pronounced incurable, having reached that stage where they could not resist the temptation to drink. Strict prohibitory measures were adopted. Any one suspected and accused of selling intoxicating drinks was to be tried, and, if convicted, hanged forthwith. Any one found drunk was to be hanged straightway without trial. Two purveyors of liquor were hung, five inebriates suffered the same penalty, and the remaining nine hundred and ninety-five incurables overcame their irresistible tendency to drink. We should now regard these measures as extreme and harsh, but their wisdom at that time was attested by the complete eradication of intemperance. Our neighboring nation, where the evil was so much deeper seated and widespread, had, of course, to adopt less stringent measures. But their former prohibitory policy of persecuting the dealer in intoxicants, and petting the consumer, was abandoned. Both were made a party to the crime, and suffered the same penalties, and their curse of intemperance gradually disappeared.

"The war was not without its beneficial results. The time, energy and money which had heretofore been expended by the defeated nation on foreign missions were now directed to the moral needs of their own people. They had learned much of the invading army. They realized that the right, even when trammeled with a materialistic religion, was more powerful than error espoused by a true (?) religion. On our part, our soldiers had brought back wonderful stories of the progress in art and science that the Macarians* had made. They also told of the many noble deeds they had witnessed on the part of their soldiers and citizens; of the refinement and culture and nobility of those who were truly imbued with the spirit of their peculiar religion. Our philosophers and statesmen, ever liberal and progressive, concluded from these reports that we had not attached sufficient importance to the religion of our sister nation. Their religion, no doubt, contained the germs of vital truths, as well as our own ancient religions. Our own Creeto had taught a brotherhood of mankind, a sympathy and love between all of humankind, a doing unto others as we should wish to be done by, very unlike the antagonistic attitude which our upper and lower classes maintained towards each other. Perhaps our neighbor's religion might supply the missing principles, or moral force, that would vitalize our Creeto's teachings, and reconcile the clashing interests of labor and capital. Inasmuch as the

* So called from their prophet, Macah.

Macarians believed that we were emanations from the divine substance, to be again reabsorbed by it, and that this condition was one of peaceful oblivion, they were in harmony with our own religion and the actual nature of things. But theirs was only a partial perception of the truth, as they did not see that in the very nature of things we must of necessity come out of that peaceful oblivion and play our parts on the stage of life as before. But they did not regard this body we possess as the true self, nor the body of the universe as the true God, as we did. According to the Macarians, the real I, the true ego, was a spark, caught at our creation from the divine spiritual being that made and controlled the universe; and this divine spark or soul resided with us, as our personality, through all the changes of the material body. Our philosophers had asked them how their deity could be one in substance and yet be made up in part of such dissimilar sparks as were exhibited by the various personalities of humanity? They answered that the dissimilarity was in the visible tabernacles, the bodies, alone; that the souls, disrobed of the vile bodies, were in no wise different from one another, except in so far as that two or more divine sparks exactly alike are not the same, or identical.

"Our philosophers felt that they had not probed quite deep enough into the constitution of the universe. They believed that this doctrine of a single divine substance, which had been a leading tenet of a great religion, must represent some cosmical truth. Matter had been reduced by our scientists to seven hundred different ultimate elements. Time and again in the past it had been thought that matter had been reduced to final elements, only to find later on that these final elements were reducible to two or more elements. Up to the time that matter was supposed to consist of two hundred elements, its reduction was thought to tend towards differentiation of the parts, but thereafter each new reduction showed the new elements to be less dissimilar, and the seven hundred elements possessed far greater resemblance to one another than the two hundred had. Researches in another direction had demonstrated that a great proportion of the variety witnessed in phenomena was due to peculiarities of motion of the parts, and did not depend on the parts themselves being different. Putting these two facts together, science declared that matter in its ultimate state was homogeneous, that is, consisted of atoms all alike. This was the declaration for which philosophy had been waiting. It was now easy to comprehend the truths our neighbors' religion represented. The Universe-god was still supreme, the All, the One. The I, or ego, or personality, was one of the ultimate atoms of this Universe-god, was, in fact, the divine spark or soul caught from the divine substance. To this the Macarian philosophers cheerfully assented until, a few years later, our scholars began to press the logical consequences of the truth. If our personalities were divine sparks, so were the personalities of animals, plants, even the atoms in the dead inanimate stone were divine also. Their philosophers raised a great cry against this.

It was to make them no better than the despised animal, the stupid plant, the filthy dirt, they contended.
Our philosophers could not understand why these
people, who enjoyed so many advantages over the
lower forms of existence, should imagine themselves
reduced to their level by a simple admission of the
truth. Much less could they understand the morbid
desire for superiority and dominion over all other
creatures that their childish objections to the truth
implied. But while the Macarians stormed against
our ideas, our philosophers, with humility and earnest purpose, were only too willing to accept their
ideas and incorporate them into our own philosophy.
As their doctrine of the divine spark stood for a great
cosmical truth (more fully expounded under theorem
third of Certology), so also might their doctrine of
the transmigration of souls."   .

Here the auroraphone ceased ticking. We had
asked a great many questions and the above had
been received much more slowly than it is told. One
of the men from the house had brought our midnight
lunch, and it had been disposed of so long ago that it
was now a pleasant memory. In fact, it was near
morning, and we remembered that the thirty-six hours
of favorable conditions were up, and that three days
must now elapse before we should again hear from
Saturn. We returned to the house and had an early
breakfast. During the meal we planned our return
trip to look after our teams. By the mountain road
it would take us at least five days to make the round
trip. Mr. Lesage insisted on our return so earnestly

that we could not refuse him, though, in fact, we had no desire to do so. Through the cavern we could make the journey in three days and so be back in time to take up the thread of Mr. Bozar's narrative. While we caught two hours' sleep, Mr. Lesage's men made us a long, light ladder with which to climb the wall at the lower end of the cavern. It would be rather inconvenient to carry, but the time saved would more than compensate for the extra labor. Two hours after breakfast we were *en route*, feeling rather the worse from our interrupted sleep. When we arrived at the "Tourists' Bath" we experienced some difficulty in climbing the incline after reaching the top of the wall by means of the ladder. However, we had brought our rope, and Jim, having first tied one end of it around his body, crawled on his hands and knees to the pit by which we had entered. He threw the rope over the log and made it fast, so that the rest of us had the rope to assist us in the ascent. We soon made our way out through the two ante-rooms and hastened to our camp, which we reached just at dark. We found everything as we had left it. Our teams were comfortable and had not suffered in the least. The following day we started out to find Mr. Pardee with a view to placing our wagons and teams under his care. We found his ranch but he had not yet returned from his bear hunt. His son, a bright handsome lad of fifteen, offered to take charge of our property until his father returned. We endeavored to fix upon the price of his services with his mother, who, though still confined to her bed, was very talkative and hospitable, telling us their history from the time they filed their claim in '65, up to the present, and urging us to make ourselves at home, but stoutly refusing to accept any compensation for the favor we asked. Telling "Bub," as he was called, that we should pay him for his trouble, we returned for the wagons and teams, the lad accompanying us. His alacrity and skill, in helping to harness and hitch up, convinced us that our property would be in the hands of a safe and zealous guardian. The wagons were left in the yard near the house, and the teams turned into a large pasture, to make friends with a bronco and milch cow, this being all the stock that the hunter possessed. Besides Bub and the "kid," there was another child, a little girl of twelve years, with all her father's beauty and frankness. Rose—and a little mountain rose-bud she was—proved a capable assistant to Bub, leading the two horses to pasture while he took charge of the mules. We started on our return trip to the "retreat" early in the morning of the third day, and late in the afternoon we were again thrilling with the grand strains of the orchestra. At dark we were once more enjoying Mr. Lesage's hospitality and praising Pete's divine cooking. It must not be supposed from the omission to record the fact that we had missed any meals during our absence. Three square meals a day had formed pleasant breaks in the monotony of the trip. Just how we enjoyed those meals can be fully appreciated only by pedestrians who for twelve hours a day have gathered oxygenated

mountain air in the stalactitic intricacies of phospho-
rescently illuminated caverns.

During our absence a rude pole-house had been
constructed over the auroraphone and furnished with
a camp stove and chairs, so that we should be more
comfortable henceforth in our attendance on the wonderful instrument.

A little after dark we repaired to the summit. A
thunderstorm was raging in the valley to the east of
us, and it was not until it had subsided that we got
an answer to our repeated calls to Saturn. After explaining that the electrical storm (indicating that the
atmosphere was overcharged with electricity, which
interfered with the natural currents) delayed his communication, Mr. Bozar continued his story:

"In addition to its inability to remedy the labor
troubles," he said, "our religion had another defect:
it did not meet the demand for simple justice. As it
then stood, the immortality which it assured us
seemed unjust, though as it was clearly the decree of
the God-universe, it was deemed irreverent to question
God's wisdom and justice in establishing such an
order of things. Scepticism, however, had long been
boldly declaring that a god who would doom the poor
and suffering of humanity to one round of hopeless
sorrow throughout all eternity was guilty of gross
injustice. That we should all live again, the rich and
happy to glide through their joyful experiences, the
poor and miserable to grope through their weary
round of toil and pain, was not questioned by the
skeptics. The nonsense of believing in any just and

beneficent Power in the face of these facts was the point they made. The doctrine of an intermediate state between death and our reproduction had never been taught. The inconceivable stretch of time (required to work out every possible combination of atoms) which must elapse between death and our restoration to life was supposed to be a peaceful blank. As we were ourselves by virtue of our peculiarly combined atoms, there could be no resurrection until this peculiar combination of atoms was again effected. During the succeeding cycle of the universe, there would be living beings as in the present cycle, but as the various elements must necessarily be differently combined, there could be no identity of individuals until billions and billions of cycles had exhausted every different combination possible. But now the homogeneity of matter, and the doctrine of the divine spark, or ultimate-atom personality called for a modification of our religion, and the Macarians' theory of the transmigration of souls seemed to contain the germ of the new cosmical truth to be learned.

"The first deduction from homogeneity was that the phenomena of each succeeding cycle would be identical with the phenomena of the present cycle, in fact, identical with all preceding cycles—atoms all alike combining under the same force must produce a succession of the same results. A further conclusion f.om the eternal activity of the universe was now necessitated—the universal exchange of the relative positions of the ultimate atoms. No activity could occur except by incessant change of atoms from one place to another. True, in great epochs constituting great cycles, every atom must stand in the same relation to all other atoms that it does in the present cycle. But while each cycle is a repetition of some remote cycle, yet it is a change from the cycle immediately preceding it."

We here "called" Saturn and asked for a more lucid explanation, not forgetting, however, to make the request very "respectfully."

"For illustration," clicked the auroraphone, "let us suppose the universe to contain but six atoms all alike, which we shall name A, B, C, D, E and F. The only phenomenon produced during a cycle is a man composed of these six atoms — head, body, two arms and two legs. During the present cycle A is the head, B the body, C, D, arms, E, F, legs. During the next cycle the same man is produced, for there are the same atoms and the same force to combine them; but now A is an arm, B the head, etc. If A experienced certain sensations by being the head, so now B, by being the head, will experience A's sensations in every particular. The relative positions of the atoms are all changed during each cycle, and finally A will have come around to be head again. Now we multiply the atoms and phenomenon by two, so we have two men and twelve atoms. Before A, starting as the head of the first, shall regain that position, he must have been the head, body, arms and legs of the second man, while the atoms of the second man must undergo a change of position with the atoms of the first man. The two men are produced at each recurring cycle, taking twelve cycles in this simple case before a repetition of the first positions occurs or a great cycle is completed. But while the twelfth cycle is a repetition of the cycle twelve cycles back, yet it is different from the cycle immediately preceding it, for, during the eleven cycles, A has not been the head of the first man, but has been filling the eleven other positions of this twelve-fold universe. Now, with a universe of homogeneous atoms, and some certain one of these atoms being our personality or soul, it was evident that this personality, the *I*, must become the personality, the *I* of every organism developed, plant, animal and human, and so the universal and complete transmigration of souls must be admitted. During every cycle the same organisms, the same general results, the same succession of events will be produced, but there will have been a change of personality. In course of time I shall have acted as the personality of every living organism, shall have experienced every sensation, shed every tear, felt every pain, thrilled with every joy that the vast universe has known. Thus there is not only the brotherhood of mankind, but the onehood of all existence. The divine-spark or ultimate-atom personality is no less itself by being incorporated in another organism as its personality. In time, as the personality of your organism, I shall know and feel all you have known and felt; you, your real self, your ego, will come to inhabit my organism and know and feel all I have known and felt. Though so far apart we are virtually one. The Permutation of

Personality, as we call it, is now so clearly expounded and proved under theorem fourth of Certology, that we wonder at the doubt and perplexity it once occasioned.

"The truth once propounded and understood, our people accepted it in spirit and in truth. The skeptics, realizing the supreme justice of the Universe-god, became its most devout worshipers. Pessimists who had doubted the wisdom and justice of God from the facts of evil and misery, now became the loudest in their praise of the cosmic deity, and its exact justice to all. Long ago a sect had taught that the good and virtuous, at death, were transported to a heavenly region to enjoy uninterrupted happiness; the wicked to be doomed to uninterrupted misery. The happiness and suffering of these two classes, however, could not be defined as in any way differing from the happiness and suffering of the present. Science had demonstrated that happiness and suffering were relative, the one dependent on the other. A condition of uninterrupted happiness, no matter how various and dissimilar the causes which produce it, if long continued, must finally result in unconsciousness. No suffering no pleasure, is the true statement. Every thrill of pleasure is possible only in contrast to some throe of pain, the latter suffered in part by the individual, in part by ancestors, in part by those with whom he is surrounded. Evil and suffering are thus as essential to a life worth living as are virtue and pleasure; so the justice and wisdom and goodness of the Universe-god is in no wise jeopardized by the presence of crime and misery in the world. If one individual or generation bears a greater burden than another, during one cycle of the universe, yet in some future cycle, by the permutation of personality, they reap their reward.

"The great expansion of sympathy and love which the new doctrine occasioned now began to bear fruit. The dissatisfaction and hatred with which the poor had regarded the rich gave way to content, when they remembered that the very advantages which they had so often looked upon with envy and bitterness must in the eternal justness and fitness of things be their own. On the other hand, the rich, when they realized that all the wretchedness, hopelessness, ignorance and degradation of the poor must ultimately be their own, found their complacency and arrogance giving way to sympathy, which expressed itself in deeds of charity and kindness. Both classes remembered the sufferings of ancestors who had toiled and fought and died for the liberty we now enjoyed. A new inspiration was given in the thought that every effort toward a better life was so much toward repaying the martyrs of the past. Every advance made, every triumph over wrong, every step toward morality, would benefit not only ourselves, but every creature in existence, or that ever has been in existence. With such motives for action, our nation in an incredibly short time was like one vast family where all was sympathy, kindness and love. Peace and prosperity reigned. The people were so universally happy and contented that we began to believe that ours was the superior planet of all the universe, and our nation the greatest and wisest on our planet. Such a millennium-like condition, we thought, was only possible at the apex of progression.

"Mechanical devices had been brought to a marvelous degree of perfection. With the discovery of matal, a material strong as steel and light as cork, machines that it had been thought impossible to make were constructed with ease. Air ships and flying machines were as common as electrical road-carts had been previous to the discovery of matal. Although we supposed that the desire to have dominion over some one of our own kind had long been suppressed, yet machinery, as it approached perfection, began to assume the human form. The most efficient machines were made in the semblance of man. Such perfection was attained in this direction that all the ordinary labor was done by these human-like machines. Every man had his duplicate in matal—delicate wheels, cogs and little giant springs. Later they performed the most difficult work, and filled positions of the greatest responsibility. They made the most efficient soldiers, the best accountants, the safest bank cashiers. Other nations are using these inventions and adding to their usefulness. For years our wars were carried on with these dummies for soldiers. At first officers superintended in person all the marches and military manœuvres. Then, in time, the officers' dummies were competent to take charge of the mechanical troops, while the officers merely superintended the men who charged the dummies. These latter are propelled by small but powerful

9

electromoters which from time to time have to be re-
charged. Certain laws governed the capture and destruction of these automatic soldiers. But wars have
long ago become obsolete, and all civil and interna-
tional difficulties are settled by arbitration.

"Military operations with dummies is now our
national game. Boys play at it for health and recreation. Professionals engage in it for profit and
fame. All classes take great interest in it, and it affords a great deal of wholesome and pleasant excitement and amusement.

"We have constantly progressed, all forgetful of the
fact that progress is constantly generating forces
which if not guarded against end in retrogression.
We have converted all the nations of Saturn to our
form of government, which is a republic, and to our
religion—faith in the permutation of personality, and
that as we do unto others so shall we be done by.
This was not done by force of arms nor by sending
missionaries to other countries. Our zeal was all
spent at home in the cause of humanity,—righting
wrongs, teaching the love of justice, the practice of
morality, and a broad sympathy for human-kind.
Our success was so great that other countries sent
their wise men to us to learn the truths and principles
that had wrought such harmony and love among our
people. Our philosophers and statesmen had decided
that that would be the speediest way to evangelize
the world, and so it has proved to be. Ours was a
true religion, and its spirit and power spread abroad,
through those who came from every land to carry

home the same good principles of justice and sympathy that have lifted us to our present greatness.

"I have hurried this communication very much in order to bring our history down to the present hour. You will now better understand the great calamity which has overtaken us in the past two days—our time. The latest improvement in the dummy is an adjustment whereby it charges its own electrometer, making it entirely independent of help or supervision from owners or attendants. Thus humanity has been relieved of all labor whatever. For years our attention has been given to pleasure and to moral and intellectual improvements, to the neglect of all the useful arts of building, cooking and tailoring. By means of pleasant recreation and the wonderful progress of medical science we have guarded against any depreciation of the general health, the only penalty, as we thought, that could possibly result from the abandonment of labor. But how fearfully were we mistaken! Those fiendish dummies, after all our pains to create them, have proved themselves most ungrateful wretches. They are all on a strike, every man, woman and child of them. Not a peaceful strike, but an armed revolt. We cannot understand it at all, nor did we ever dream of the possibility of such a thing. They cannot possibly have any motive. They possess no feeling. They have absolutely nothing to gain by it. Still we cannot rail at them in reason. They are our own creations, and had we been content to continue the mere trifle of labor necessary to charge them, they would still be under our control, use-

ful and obedient servants. But as it is we are as helpless as children in the hands of giants. Communications from all over the world state that the uprising
is general and preconcerted, the intent being to overthrow all government. In the great square just outside our city's walls, where our military games take
place, the dummies are drilling, their banners flying,
drums beating, and bugles blowing. They have taken
nearly all of the arms belonging to the city. Their
messengers are seen going and coming to and from
other cities. We have closed the massive gates, which
makes the city practically safe for the time being. As
the gates close, a net-work of wires connected with
powerful batteries spreads over the city, so that any
attempt to gain an entrance by flying machines will
prove fruitless. Quite a body of dummies had been
stationed to guard the gates, and only by surprising
them with an overwhelming force of old-fashioned
dummies that had long ago been laid aside because
they needed to be charged, were we enabled to gain
the gates. Many of our citizens had to participate in
the struggle and several were slain, the first blood
shed in war for years. The outlook is very serious indeed. One thing is certain, the world is on the eve of
one of the most terrible conflicts ever known. More of
our people will fall than in all the wars of the past.
The dummies are unfeeling, tireless, swift, strong, well
disciplined, and have the best officers, and nearly all
the arms. Our only hope is that we may hit upon
some military tactics that they are not adjusted to
meet. Many cities are without walls or protection of

any kind, and their citizens have been compelled to flee to mountains and other cities for refuge. Thousands and thousands of them have been intercepted and slain while fleeing to fortified cities for protection.

"The 'Hourly News' ascribes the revolt to the universal tendency to blindly exercise a superior power, just for the sake of exercising it. It further takes the ground that this is but the reaction of a superior power used ages ago, when the upper classes kept the lower, ground down for no other cause than that they could do it. It cites the fact, in support of its position, that so soon as a more sympathetic policy was adopted, the condition of the wealthy was greatly improved, to say nothing of the improved condition of the poor. It further holds that we must learn from this, if indeed any of us are spared, that men, as nations or as individuals, cannot cease to engage in manual labor. A certain amount of useful labor with the hands, daily performed, it maintains, is the price to be paid for immunity from such bloody calamities as the one which now threatens to sweep the human race from the face of our planet. By the inconvenience of labor, or the pain of daily exertions put forth to the production of some useful thing, it contends, those destructive forces which are constantly generated in the course of progress will be met and overcome, while they are isolated and weak — before they unite and grow into irresistible waves to overwhelm us.

"But I see it is again morning with you, and as I am detailed to stand guard for two hours I must now go. I shall get four hours' rest, and will be here at your service at the noon hour, as you count time."

Filled with deep concern for our Saturnian friends we made our way to the house. We found breakfast ready and Pete in attendance. He was very uncommunicative and seemed absorbed with some great resolve of his own, though it was only after learning the fact that we so interpreted his mood. We lost an hour or so of much needed sleep in discussing the probable termination of the dummies' revolt. However, we slept away the most of the forenoon. At twelve Pete awaked us for dinner, and after placing the meal on the table withdrew and left us to wait on ourselves. We hurried through the meal, so anxious were we to learn of the condition of affairs in the faraway planet, and at half past twelve we started up the trail. When about two thirds the way up, we met Pete hurrying down. There was a look of exultation on his face that at once aroused our fears for the safety of the auroraphone. His first words confirmed them, but not as we expected.

"No use to go up dar any mo', Marse Gaston," he said: "I done made sho' de ole debil wa' gwine to get yo', an' I says, 'Pete, yo' jes' got to save Marse Gaston. The good book says to resist de debil an' he will flee frum yo'. So I jes' goes to dat telegraph'n' 'sheen an' sends ole Beelzebub er telegram myse'f. 'Yo' ole debil,' says I, 'jes' get clar behind me an' neber let me see yo' talk'n' to Marse Gaston agin.' Arter I done tole 'im what's what I come away pow'ful sud'n, fear'n' de ole cus would try to palaver me."

We remembered with a thrill of terror what we had been told in regard to being respectful in our communications. With one accord we whirled around and essayed to rush down the trail. But at that instant there was a blinding flash of light, a terrific crash, and I knew no more for several minutes. I was recalled to consciousness by Pete, who had first recovered from the shock, calling on Mr. Lesage to wake up. He was doing all within the compass of his powerful voice to restore the old gentleman to consciousness, but to no purpose. When I looked around the others were sitting up, but still too bewildered to render any assistance to Pete. In a few moments, however, we were all doing our utmost to aid Pete in his endeavors to arouse Mr. Lesage, but our united exertions produced no signs of life. We constructed a rude litter and carried him to the house. After an hour's chafing of his body, he was breathing freely but still unconscious. Pete, up to the time that Mr. Lesage showed unmistakable signs of life, had been very attentive, but afterwards kept himself aloof from the sick room. He was evidently in great fear of the reckoning which must come when his employer should recover.

When Mr. Lesage was found to be resting easily, we left him in care of his men and made our way to the summit to see what damage had been done. The pole house and auroraphone were scattered about in atoms. A great fissure marked the place where they had stood. The charge of electricity had ploughed through the lake and into the cavern, filling the entrance with a mass of rock that would take years to remove. Pete's little knowledge of telegraphy had worked havoc and destruction beyond the power of man to repair. We should be only too glad to see the settlement between Pete and his employer, when the latter should learn of the destruction of his instrument.

It was not until the following day that Mr. Lesage learned of the ruin that had been worked. On hearing the particulars, he smiled grimly and asked for Pete. Pete, immediately after breakfast that morning, had taken an axe and gone probably a mile away to chop fire-wood. He realized that he was at the bottom of the mischief, and his concern, now, was not so much for his employer's deliverance from Satan as for his own temporal welfare. I went after Pete, as I was not loath to witness his misery when he knew he had to face Mr. Lesage. Guided by the sound of his axe I had no trouble to find him. He guessed my errand, I judged from his lugubrious countenance as I came up to him. "Mr. King," I said, addressing him by his surname, "Mr. Lesage has a little matter of business to discuss with you and begs that you will grant him the honor of a personal interview."

"Wha—what's dat, Boss, Marse Gaston a cussin'?"

"Mr. Lesage wants to see you in his room."

"Now, look a hyar, Boss," said Pete, pulling out an old greasy wallet, "Yo' jes' tell Marse Gaston dat I neber know'd de debil wa' gwine to flar' up so mighty huffy-like er I wouldn't neber said nuf'n' to 'im, an' dat I's mighty sorry he's lost his telegraph'n' 'trivance. I's willin' ter pay Marse Gaston ebery cent I got in de worl' and wo'k fo' 'im all de rest ob my days ter boot. I's sabed up two hundr'd an' fo'ty dolla's an' yo' jes' take 'em to Marse Gaston and tell 'im ole Pete wishes it wa' mo'."

"As Mr. Lesage had about thirty-five thousand dollars invested in the instrument," I replied, "he will think your offer a munificent one indeed!"

"I know it's nuf'n' at all to Marse Gaston," Pete responded, "but it's a mighty big pile er money to me, an' Marse Gaston knows I'd give him mo' ef I had it."

"Well," I answered, "you must go and see Mr. Lesage yourself, and if you can convince him that your few dollars will repay the loss he has suffered through you, perhaps he will not have us hang you after all."

"Oh, I know Marse Gaston's not gwine to hurt ole Pete. It's wus'n dat. He'll jes' say, 'I no mo' use fo' yo', nigger, an' I can jes' clar out an' git. Dat's what'll kill dis yer chile, but I knows dat's jes' what't'll come to, an' I can't blame Marse Gaston nohow."

When we arrived at the house we went directly to Mr. Lesage's room. He was sitting in a large easy-chair talking with the boys, who had assembled to see Pete get his just deserts. Pete, without saying a word, or even looking at his employer, sat down in a chair near the door.

"I have sent for you, Pete," said Mr. Lesage, in a voice the gentleness of which surprised and disappointed us, "to thank you for the kindly interest you have taken in my eternal welfare. I am pained and distressed, not at the loss of the instrument, but at the loss of the respect and confidence of the people of another world; still I have not been angry at you, old friend." Pete for the first time looked up, more surprised than any of us. "On the contrary," continued Mr. Lesage, I appreciate the moral courage you have shown in your concern for another. Probably none of us, with the same fear of that instrument, and believing in its direct connection with the Evil One, would have had the courage to face it as you did in behalf of one we loved. I wonder how you accomplished it, for you must have been terribly frightened."

"I war scared pow'ful bad," broke in Pete, "an' my knees jes' shook an' knocked togedder so hard dat dey mighty so' yit," and he began to rub the subjects of his exaggeration; "but I 'membered what de good book says about facin' de debil an' I jes' walked up to 'im quick and tole 'im as how he'd got to let you alone. But I swa' to grashus, Marse Gaston, I neber know'd ole Satan gwine to get his back up like dat and bust tings all to flinders, an' nearly knock the life out'n all of us besides."

"Don't make any excuses, Pete," Mr. Lesage answered. "We have learned wonderful things of him whom you mistake to be Satan; and even if you had not had such good intentions we could but forgive you; for one of the things we have learned is that we must all be you, in time, and then we shall appreciate your motives, and know how pleasant it will be to be held blameless. So, old friend, be entirely at ease and try to realize that I have greater affection for you than ever."

"Does you really mean it for sho', Marse Gaston, an' ain't Pete got to go arter all?" Pete asked in astonishment and doubt.

Mr. Lesage again assured him of the fact, stating that he had been taught the best of all motives for doing unto others as he wished to be done by.

"Well den," Pete answered, as he affectionately took one of the hands he had so tirelessly chafed the day before, "dar was jes' no debil about it at all. If dat's what yo' been taut it's de good Lawd an' not Satan what yo' been telegraph'n' to, an' ole Pete's been a big fool. Wonder he didn't smash me erlong wid de roryfone for callin' 'im de ole debil."

Mr. Lesage explained to Pete that he was only following the general rule in being frightened into thinking that a most beneficent discovery of science was the work of the devil. Mr. Lesage's conduct had been a timely and gentle reprimand to the rest of us. We now began to realize the full import of the teachings we had been receiving from Saturn. Would I, indeed, in some future age be Pete? Would the I, or Ego, which now receives its impressions through a white skin, blue eyes, and Caucasian brain, in some distant cycle be incorporated in that dusky form, knowing as its own sensations all of Pete's impressions? It seemed impossible. Pete, too, had been thinking about this matter, for suddenly he broke out into a guffaw as only a darkey can, possessed with a funny idea.

"Marse Gaston," he asked between his explosions, "what's dat you said about being ole black Pete? I's gwine to belebe ebery ting yo' tells me now, but dat's a pow'ful uncom'n idee. Haw! haw! haw!"

Mr. Lesage, who was already a convert to the strange theory, assumed the responsibility of assuring Pete that he, Mr. Lesage, would become Pete in the course of time. He talked to the colored man in a very earnest and impressive manner, but Pete, to whom the idea grew funnier the better he understood it, only responded with renewed guffaws, ending in a prolonged yell when his ordinary means of express-ing his mirth failed him. When Pete's risibility had expended itself, Mr. Lesage improved the occasion to impress upon him the further fact that he, Pete, must become Mr. Lesage. His earnestness left no room for doubt in Pete's mind; but this idea, rather strangely, did not appeal to the comic side of his nature. But again he questioned, more to be confirmed than to ex-press doubt: "Marse Gaston, yo' say I'm gwine to be yo'?"

"Yes."

"An' gwine to be white an' know how to read and write, an' all yo' knows yo'se'f? There was a ring of hope in his voice, and eyes and face expressed deep awe at this strange fact. It was the reawakening of hopes and desires which for generations had been smothered out at their very birth — the hope and de-sire to be otherwise than one of an inferior race, the longing to overstep the chasm that nature seemed to have fixed between them and the race that enjoyed all the superior advantages of life. Pete's sparkling eyes and glowing face, as Mr. Lesage again assured him of his final transformation, were a study. Looking at Pete, there thrilled through me the conviction that the strange theory did express God's own eternal justice.

Later in the day Mr. Lesage told us of his intention to set up his other instrument on the site of the one destroyed, and pass the remainder of his days in waiting for a renewal of our suddenly interrupted communications with Saturn. To our minds the prompt and terrific manner of expressing their displeasure seemed to indicate that a very long period of silence would be maintained by the people of Saturn; but Mr. Lesage thought, or at least hoped, that but a few years would elapse before we should hear from them again.

The second day following the calamity, we bid farewell to our kind friends of the "retreat," and in due time reached the hunter's ranch where we had left our teams.

"Sim" had returned, and our talk as we approached the house brought him to the door, and from thence to the yard to meet us. One of his arms was in a sling and the hand of the other was bandaged. A cloth was wound around his head, and another passed under his chin and was knotted on top of his head. His face was nearly obscured with plasters, but such portions as peeped out fairly beamed with "peace and quiet." He greeted us with his characteristic abruptness:

"I found the bar—biggest one, sure 'nough, ever killed in these yer parts. Thort he'd everlastingly chaw me into mince meat, but I guess I made 'em sick at ther stumick. I'm getting on all right. Nothing

like a good mother-in-law to pull a feller through after
a tussle with a bar. Mammy's cooking up some of
the best bits, and you must stay to dinner. Come
right in and see the kid, and git acquainted."

The invitation of seven hungry boys to dinner
spoke volumes for his hospitality, and, as there was
no refusing him, we "staid to dinner." The "kid," a
tiny bit of humanity, was passed around and introduced as Nellie Pardee. By the time this formality
was through with, dinner was announced, and with
the aid of five boxes we were all seated at the long
rough table that had been placed in the center of the
one room. The table was spread with a cloth the like
of which I had never seen before. It was made of gunny-
sacks which had been sewed together, washed and
bleached to a show of whiteness. By this I identified
the material of Rose's single garment, and of Bub's
shirt and trowsers. The meal was very frugal, bear's
meat, gravy, corn bread, and water. It was poverty,
far out of proportion to the hunter's strength and
the possibilities of the splendid ranch he owned, but
had not developed. Again I found myself thinking
about the transmigration of souls. I wondered if I
should, some time in the future, be the lazy, good natured, thriftless and yet courageous hunter. The
prospect was not a pleasant one to contemplate, even
though my advantages were not strikingly different
from Mr. Pardee's. And here there seemed to be a defect in the Creetan theory of soul-transformation.
When contemplating those more fortunately situated,
or even in contemplating the hope it awakened in

those less fortunately situated, as in Pete's case, it was easy to believe the theory. But when I was called on to entertain the belief that I must become the personality of all lower forms of existence, it seemed to be carrying the principle of democracy rather too far. And yet why did I shrink from this phase of the theory? My conscience would answer that my antipathy was but the hostility of the natural man — the selfish part of my nature, to divine justice. Why all these lower forms of existence — forms of ignorance, crime, and suffering — unless they served some beneficent end in the economy of the universe? If they were the price of the higher forms of existence, intelligence, pleasure, morality, why should not I pay the price, instead of enjoying the blessings that others have purchased? Surely God had legislated in my favor. By some divine decree I was better than a great portion of my fellow creatures. It was the pleasanter thought, and I hugged it close to my bosom. Again, so far from tending to morality, would not the theory work a contrary result? Once satisfied that some distant cycle would bring us to a more desirable tabernacle, and to more pleasant conditions, would we not be inclined to yield ourselves to fate and let matters take their natural course with the least possible help or hindrance from our hands? But if I accepted the theory, by the same process of reasoning, just used, it would follow that I should sit down and no longer be moved by hunger or cold to activity. No, I could not reject the theory on that ground. Were I to accept the theory, all my incentives to action would still remain. I was already regarding these poor people with deeper interest just from having heard of the theory, and, no doubt, all through life, every instance of wretchedness, misery and crime that should come under my notice would excite a kindlier feeling in me for suffering humanity. But granting this—that the thought of being in the sufferer's place does awaken a keener sympathy for my fellow-creatures,—was it not likely to lower the standard of morality? Wrong doing was perhaps at the bottom of all the distress, and it would be better to have some theory to harden my heart against the sight of misery. My reason said, Let them starve and freeze and steal and kill, but look carefully to your own moral welfare, and you will have done your duty. There was no great degree of satisfaction following this conclusion, but that would come when the novelty of the theory had worn off.

Occupied with these thoughts I lost nearly all of the talk during the meal. We managed to pay the family for our dinners and for the care of our teams. Bub was made the recipient of five bright silver dollars. We drove up to Wagon Wheel Gap that afternoon, and with concentrating all our care on our health for a few weeks, we thought less of the events of the past few days than we otherwise should. Still it was an every-day occurrence during our stay there and on our way back to Colorado Springs, to wonder how the dummies' revolt would be suppressed by the good people of Saturn.

BOOK II.

TEN YEARS LATER.

CHAPTER VI.

PLEASANT REUNIONS.

TEN years have passed away since I parted with my six friends at Colorado Springs — years that have brought to me many sorrows and cares. 1889 found me living in one of the "boom" smitten cities of Western Kansas, ostensibly in the mercantile trade but virtually waiting for the country to recover from the great collapse of '87. In the spring of the latter year the great gambling epidemic raged in our midst, and by many of us legitimate business was deemed too slow, and left to take care of itself, while every available dollar was invested in real estate — real estate that in a few weeks was to realize us a handsome fortune, but which instead could not be disposed of at any price.

One sultry afternoon in July, '89, I was busily engaged in my store, — on a gloomy retrospection; so absorbed, in fact, was I with the dismal phantoms, that I was but vaguely conscious of the shadow which had darkened the doorway. Some transactions of the past two years, I was thinking, were possibly not so great mistakes as others. I was confronted, however, with various shades of wrong judgment and mismanagement, all of an unmistakable indigo tint. The picture in my mind would have been termed by artists a discord in blue. To my mind it was a distressing fit of the blues. Just as the sombre-hued thoughts were about to express themselves in an agonizing groan, a voice from the doorway yelled, "Git!" and the haunting spectres were put to flight as precipitately as had been the supposed horse thieves ten years before, by the eloquence of that voice. It was my cousin Mel, hale, hearty and jolly, an M.D. now of several years' practice. He had started in on an already thinly populated community and had, of course, by this time to look up a new location. He had found the place in the central part of the Sunflower State, and had run out to make me a visit before settling down to practice in his new field. Mel was a bachelor, thirty-one years old, strong, prosperous and happy. I was a bachelor, thirty years old, in poor health, bankrupt and gloomy. The cheerful companionship of my cousin was a boon to me just at that time, and fortunately it was continued beyond our expectations.

By a coincidence, not strange to those who regard all things as directed by law, the first mail from the west after Mel's arrival brought the following letter to me.

MOUNTAIN RETREAT, COLO., July 18-89.
MR. S. I. KARBUN.

Dear Sir and Friend: You will be glad to know that my patient waiting has at last been rewarded. A message came yesterday from Saturn. It appears that our friend Mr. Bozar has disappeared, presumably killed by the dummies during the great revolt ten years ago. The Saturnians have only lately found a record of a "communication with the people of Opak" and nothing to show "the status of it." The message I received also states that they will make a more thorough search among the public records, for further particulars, and also make careful inquiries concerning Mr. Bozar. Failing to find anything more in regard to the matter, they propose to renew the correspondence where it was broken off, as per their record, which brings their history up to the second day of the revolt. I am to hear from them in twelve days at all events.

I am confident that we shall resume friendly relations with the distant planet, and as we shall now be in constant communication with its citizens we may make known to the world the things we have heard. Without this substantial proof we could not hope to make the most credulous believe the facts. But soon all may come, and see and hear for themselves. You and your friends will want to visit these beautiful mountains again, and once more enjoy one another's companionship; and as the occasion is one of such unusual interest, I am very hopeful of seeing you all here in a few days. I write to the others by this mail. Steam will now bring you to this region, though not, perhaps, so pleasantly as you once made the trip. Our own road up the mountain has been somewhat improved, and Pete himself shall be in waiting at the station to drive you to my ' retreat.''

Trusting to see you soon, I am your sincere friend,

GASTON LESAGE.

We received the letter on the morning of the 19th, and we boarded the west bound train at 4 P.M. the following day, and were borne from the hot, dusty Kansas town toward the cool smiling mountains of Colorado. A pleasant surprise awaited us at Pueblo in the person of Jim. Mr. Lesage, after writing, had immediately concluded to send telegrams to those who were the farthest away; consequently Jim had the word and was en route over the '' Missouri Pacific'' before I got my letter. Hundreds of operators are still wondering at those six queer messages that went flashing through their offices, the substance of which was as follows: '' Saturn heard from. Come immediately.''

We arrived at L., the station nearest Mr. Lesage's

home, in the middle of the afternoon of the 21st. Our great promptness had not been expected, and we were sorely disappointed in not finding Pete at the station to receive us. While the little mountain depot was strange to us, yet we recognized many familiar landmarks, and soon discovered that we were near the site of our old camping ground. It was now about three o'clock, and not expecting Pete before night, we concluded to make a call on our hunter friend, taking it for granted that he still resided at the old ranch, which was a mile distant from the station. The walk was a pleasure, but we found the ranch so wonderfully improved that we concluded that its thriftless owner of ten years before had sold out and moved to a wilder region. A large, handsome, frame building stood on the site of the old log house, and the grounds were beautiful with greensward, flowers and shrubs. A broad veranda on the front and east side of the house gave a comfortable and home-like appearance to the otherwise modern and stylish dwelling. The veranda had two occupants, a young lady and a little girl, the latter occupying a hammock, which the young lady was swinging vigorously, the child attesting its appreciation by merry peals of laughter. As we were somewhat thirsty we concluded to get a drink from the old spring, which we saw had been covered with a picturesque spring-house, and also make some inquiries concerning the former owner of the place. In answer to our request for a drink the young lady brought us a glass and directed us to the spring at the rear of the house. As we turned the

corner of the house on our way to the spring we were
met by a well dressed gentleman, who stopped short
and contemplated us for a moment, as we did him.

"Wall I swar!" exclaimed the gentleman, "if 'tain't
the youngsters 'twer here when I killed the big bar;
bless my soul if 'tain't!" and he shook hands all around
two times, as if the coincidence of our having been
there when he killed the "big bar" was the strongest
of all human ties. "War on a bar hunt," he lost no
time in saying, "over in the San Juan country a year
or so after you were here and found a silver mine,—I
did, by gracious! It panned out immense; leastwise
'twas for me. I fixed up the old place till I think it's
just scrumptious. I've edicated the children, and Rose
and Bub ain't got no ekals in larnin'; no, sir, not any-
whar on the face of the yarth. Got a pianer, too, and
you just bet Rose can everlastingly thump it. It war
wuss'n a mammy-in-law at first, and I war just driv to
hunt bar day and night. That pianer's been a regular
holycust to the bars in these parts. It would just set
me after them a ragin' and a tarin', and I'd kill three
or four 'fore I'd feel any peace and quiet at all. But
that's all over now and when Rose's to home I just
keep her playin' poorty and soft like and no bar big or
little can entice me away from home now."

This was a long talk for the hunter, but it was
all told, and beyond inviting us in to hear Rose play
we heard but little more from him. He insisted on
our staying with his 'folks' until Pete put in an appearance. It was the same irresistible appeal that
had led us to take dinner with them in the days of

their extreme poverty, and we consented to stay, perhaps for a week, with far less reluctance than we had assented to partake of that one humble meal.

The first thing was to hear Rose play, and we followed our host into the luxuriously and tastefully furnished parlor. A grand piano stood open across one corner of the room. Rose, to whom we had been introduced in a lump as the "very identical youngsters that were here when I killed the big bar," consented to play, not, it was evident, to satisfy our doubting curiosity, but to please her father, of whom she was both fond and proud. She had a sweet, clear voice which had been well cultivated, and she played with a touch and expression that no amount of practice could have mastered without great natural aptitude for music. For an hour those tireless, flexible fingers flew up and down the keyboard, filling the room with such harmonies as only the perfect master of the piano can command. It was a striking illustration of the power of wealth to bring out and develop one's natural tastes and talents. Rose's small, graceful figure was tastefully arrayed with none of that display of finery and jewels which under the circumstances might have been expected. Still her dress was a decided contrast to the coarse garment she had worn when we first saw her. But the great transformation had been in Rose herself—the change from the wonderful beauty of the child to that more wondrous thing, the beauty of a pure, sweet woman.

As I listened to the music and looked around the richly furnished room, I could but think of the time when we sat around the gunny-sack-covered table, with boxes for chairs. Then I had thought that to be in the hunter's place made the theory of a universal exchange of personalities seem a very harsh one. But then there was extreme poverty and illiteracy combined. There was illiteracy still, but in this womanly, accomplished daughter, who, it was evident, was not a bit ashamed of her parents, there was compensation for a far greater misfortune than the mere want of learning. The theory, to which I was already a professed convert, rose in my estimation as I noticed the father's look of pride and affection. Before, I had not hesitated to pronounce this man thriftless and lazy from the general appearance of neglect and dilapidation that the ranch showed, nor had I endeavored to find any excuse for him. But now, the fact that in his chosen work none were more tireless, crafty and persevering than he, seemed a great deal in his favor. He simply liked to hunt as other men, noted for industry, liked the avocations which, fortunately, yielded a living, respectability and influence. His industry had been rewarded at last, and his good fortune no more the result of accident, perhaps, than that of others.

Mrs. Pardee, who had returned from a visit to one of the neighbors, came into the room just as Rose ceased playing, and we were forthwith introduced for the second time as the youngsters who were in that vicinity on the memorable occasion of the demise of the huge bear. •

" Why, I'll declare if 'tain't some of the young

gentlemen 'twere here when Nellie was born," was the
mother's means of identifying us, and she greeted us
with a friendly fervor that left no doubt in our minds
that between Nellie and the big bear we had a claim
on this family's affections that ranked next to kin.
"Nellie's at school," continued Mrs. Pardee, "or on
the way home"—she corrected herself looking at an
elegant bronze clock on the mantel,—and it will just do
you good to see Nellie! But guess who's teaching our
school,—it's Bub; tho' pap and me's trying to learn to
call him Robert, as that's his name. He says Bub's
good 'nuff for him, and what we've always called him
we can still call him. But we know it don't sound
right and he a grown man, and before company we
always call him Robert when we don't forget and call
him Bub, which is about all the time," and she laughed
heartily at the pleasant way she had apologized
beforehand for an habitual appellation which her
mother's heart feared might, in some degree, detract
from the dignity and true worth of her first-born.
May, the little girl we had first seen in the hammock,
now claimed her mother's attention, begging permission to go and meet "Bub and Nell." Her request
granted, the little five-year-old started off in high glee.

We were sitting on the veranda, Mrs. Pardee doing
most of the talking, though Mr. Pardee had just explained that "Bub was teaching because he wasn't going to have him grow up a dude just because he'd
struck it rich," when a stalwart young man with little
May astride his neck, and Nellie, as it proved to be,
clinging to one of his hands, came into view. Bub, on

catching sight of visitors, endeavored to dislodge the child, but like Sinbad's Old Man of the Sea, she was a fixture not to be removed. Thus the trio came into the porch as we had first seen them, Bub good-naturedly confused. The mother, however, exaggerating the indignity of his situation, made haste to tear the little minx from her perch. May screamed with laughter during the scuffle, and then bawled lustily as she had to yield to superior force and was borne away by the victorious though deeply annoyed mother. The father during the struggle had stood nervously by, impatient for a chance to introduce us to the new comers with the usual reference to bruin. Bub had already recognized us and was through shaking hands by the time his father had finished the "big-bar" formula. "I remember you very distinctly," he said, laughingly, "as I date life from the time you gave me the five dollars for taking care of your teams. It was the first money I had ever had, and father's discovery of the silver mine a year later was nothing in comparison with that magnificent sum. And after all, that five dollars was the foundation of our good fortune. I hung on to my money as did the unprofitable servant who received the one talent, not willing to risk any investment to increase it. Then father, insisted on borrowing three dollars of it to buy sufficient ammunition and food to go on an extensive hunt up in the San Juan country. I yielded, not to moral suasion but to parental authority, and as a consequence father found the mine."

"And so," Mel supplemented, "we have but to say

'well done, good and faithful servant,' and receive back our own, with a hundred thousand or so for usury."

"No, that hardly follows," Bub replied: "just consider the chances I took and you will concede that your demand is out of proportion to my risks. Father could give no security, and if he hadn't made the find he would never have paid me a cent, so I should have been in a worse position than the slothful servant, for I couldn't have returned even your own. Fact is, though, father and I have often considered your claims. I contend that you furnished the 'grub stake' and have an interest in the find. Father won't recognize that as any claim at all, but says that your interest in the mine is based solely on the fact that you were here when he killed that big bear, and he expresses himself as willing to do something handsome by you. Of course I can't regard that as entitling you to any share in our good fortune, and until we get the proper ground for your claims settled between us, you must consider your cause in chancery, and be prepared to wait indefinitely for its final adjustment.

"It seems, then," Jim said, "that mere technicalities hinder us from entering into the immediate possession of our share in a silver mine?"

"No, the mine's sold," answered Mr. Pardee, "and ther money is invested in lands and houses and the fixin's you see round here. It's the improvements on this here ranch that you have an interest in as much. as any one, and ther's nothin' at all hinder'n' your takin' immegiat possession and makin' yourselves at home just as much as if you had a clar title and deed to the whole shebang."

"All right," Jim answered, "we'll camp with you a while, anyway, and if the mountain air has the same appetizing effect it had ten years ago, trust us to get more than our share of the proceeds of the five-dollar investment."

"There," Bub exclaimed, as an aroma of broiling meat reached us, "mother is about to make a payment of interest to the bondholders in this concern, and we'll soon have you clipping your coupons with a case knife."

And so the jesting went on between us. It was very pleasant to converse with this family, who laughingly referred to their former poverty, and spoke of their good fortune without any show of pride or patronage. Our talk was continued for some minutes, as there was the usual delay with the supper incident to "company," and also the unusual delay which attends such culinary preparations when the company is on the verge of starvation, as we always were in that region. Jim, who had been married a year before, had repeatedly declared that day that he had not had anything properly cooked since he left home, and was constantly drawing comparisons between the railroad eating-houses and his own establishment, greatly to the advantage of the latter. Mel and I could admire his gallantry in praising his home cooking, but we had assured him that it was utterly impossible for a wife of only one year's experience to cook anything fit to eat. We would get pretty rough usage in return on the score of our celibacy, and were rudely awakened to a sense of the crime and ignominy of bachelorhood. However, we could sympathize with his diatribes against the railroad hotel, and we were all in the best condition to enjoy good old-fashioned cooking, such as was already making the air redolent of appetizing odors.

Supper was presently announced, and it even exceeded our expectations. "There was an old-time flavor and relish to the food," as I told Mrs. Pardee, "that only the cooks of our mothers' day could impart," which seemed to please the good woman amazingly. Jim even conceded that Mrs. Pardee's old methods of cooking were superior to his wife's, telling her in his honest, sober way that while he must yield her the palm, yet she and Allie were the only two women now living that knew how to cook—that understood how to give that savoriness to food which gained our mothers such merited renown in the culinary department of every well ordered household. Our praise was honest, for the cooking was superb, "everything prepared," as Dr. Mel was assuring our hostess, "with a view to the requirements of digestion and assimilation, a quality of food rarely met with in these days of vile cooking, a quality to which no amount of lectures and hints, from the profession which I have the honor to represent, could induce modern cooks to give any attention. This is the more strange, that the cooks of the old school acquired the knack by intuition, without the aids that modern progress in physiology can now give. 'Tis a sad fact, but the art of cooking is passing away with our grandmothers, and an army of dyspeptics is sure to result," and the Doctor's face actually grew radiant at this picture of prospective patients, whereas, to coincide with the sad tone of his voice, it should have been extremely sombre and sorrowful. "Yes, Mrs. Pardee," he continued, "you are to be complimented on your skill in an art so vitally important to the human race."

"Why lawsy massy!" responded Mrs. Pardee, now that she had time to make her acknowledgments, "I can't cook fit for hogs. Rose does the cooking. She's been off to one of them industrious schools where they learn to do somethin' as well as to know something', and what Rose don't know about cookin' ain't worth learnin'."

"There, mother," said Rose, "our guests have already said enough to establish the reputation of our industrial training schools; you can't make it any more emphatic. I thank you all," she said, addressing us three crestfallen mortals, "for the honest tribute you have paid to modern methods of instruction. I must improve my vantage-ground," she continued, "and take you to task for being behind the times in not knowing—for to know is to appreciate and aid—the good work that is being done by industrial training schools. Domestic economy, of course, is of minor importance, but as you value it so highly it will be the best criterion for you to judge of the usefulness of the industrial schools. It is but natural that I should want to make friends for the system to which I am so much indebted, and I hope you will all do penance for your unkind words about present-day cooking by preaching to all your friends the gospel of labor as expounded and practiced in our manual training schools."

In truth we knew but little about industrial training as a factor in modern education, and during the meal we plied our fair critic with queries concerning it, receiving in return the information which would qualify us for the mission to which we had just been called.

After supper, Bub, as I shall continue to call him, showed us over the place. There were commodious barns and stables, some good horses and a number of fine Jersey and Holstein cows.

"We've gone into the dairy business," Bub said, "or rather mother has, as she superintends the place. Father devotes the most of his time to hunting. However, he is giving it up now that Rose is at home to stay." Although he spoke lightly, a very troubled look came over his face as he mentioned his father, but it quickly passed away. We were next shown through the spring-house and initiated into the mysteries of cream raising by means of a creamer and ice, and of butter making by the use of the most improved machinery. Two men and a hired girl constituted Mrs. Pardee's help.

On returning to the house, we found the family out on the veranda enjoying the cool of the evening. Rose was again swinging the hammock, May being the delighted occupant, while Nellie was relating some school adventure to her father and mother. We

joined the group and became busily engaged in discussing the changes of the past ten years. Rose had
disappeared into the house soon after our appearance,
but presently returned with an autograph album, and
announced that she must have our autographs. I
was selected for the first contributor. It seemed to
me that this abrupt demand for autographs savored
very much of rusticity, and I felt disappointed. I
simply subscribed my name and passed the book over
to Mel, who, seized with an interrogo-philosophical
spasm, wrote: "What am I, whence came I, and
whither am I bound?" Jim, remembering the Saturnian messages, wrote on the opposite page: "An
ultimate atom, from the Homogeneous All, and
destined for all time to describe a great circle through
all organic matter as its personality, with the plane
of affection inclined to some like personality." He
handed me the album to read his pleasantry at the
expense of a theory to which he knew I had become a
convert, and again I experienced a feeling of disappointment, this time in Jim. Still his representation
was true to the theory in every respect; and then as
he whispered, "That sizes Mel up about right, don't
it?" I perceived that his joke was directed at my
cousin, on the supposition that he had become deeply
impressed with the fair Rose. I thought it hardly
right for Jim to use the lady's album to express his
opinion on such a matter, but his meaning was so
disguised that none but the initiated could have
guessed it. Mel himself supposed it to be merely an
answer to the questions he had written, from the

11

standpoint of the theory with which we were so well acquainted, and he so explained it to Rose, which of course led to a brief statement of the theory itself, no reference, however, being made to the origin of it.

Rose and Bub presently withdrew to the farthest part of the veranda and discussed the autographs with the air of having made a discovery. Again Rose disappeared into the house, and this time returned with a little piece of cardboard. This the two carefully compared with one of the autographs. Apparently satisfied with the result, Rose suddenly pointed her finger at Mel, and exclaimed with a mock air of severity: "Thou art the man!" Mel looked extremely guilty—the more so that he was in total ignorance of the crime with which he was charged. He proved to be the culprit, however. It appeared that on arriving home ten years before, he had sent Rose a gingham dress, a pair of shoes and two pairs of stockings, which little act of anonymous charity he had entirely forgotten. Not so Rose, however. It had occurred to her that some of us had sent the gift, which, like Bub's five dollars, was the great event of her life, and she had hit on the autograph scheme to detect the donor. She had preserved the cardboard on which her name was written in Mel's elegant chirography, and further ornamented with a rose in one corner and a cute little bird in the other, because it was the nearest to a toy, Christmas card, or keep-sake that she had ever had.

But this revelation of Mel's generosity was a third disappointment to me. In fact, another one of our party had fallen a victim to the beauty and accomplishments of Rose. My disappointment was really a twinge of jealousy. I regretted very much that I had not sent the little girl something on my return home from our first trip to these mountains. It was a great deal to have won the gratitude of this charming young woman, as Mel had done by a *little* donation where it was so sorely needed. I even thought of his gift as contemptibly little, and was proceeding to censure him mentally for his littleness, when common sense checked me with the thought that I had not sent anything. This matter troubled me in another respect. While Mel had remained true to the Methodistic doctrines which had been taught us from infancy, the wonderful revelations made by our Saturnian friend, Mr. Bozar, had made me a convert to the strange theory of permutation. Mel admitted that the communications from Saturn were very remarkable, and that the history of the Saturnians might be valuable and interesting, but still these people were fallible creatures like ourselves, and for his part he "would be in no haste to accept their wild theories as gospel truths." "But they are not wild theories," I had answered, "for they say they are to them as geometrical truths are to us." Mel, however, while willing to grant their truth and honesty in this, held firmly to the belief that further discoveries on their part would explode their "certological facts." I had replied somewhat testily that it was to be supposed that we should ourselves, by and by, find that twice two does not make four, and so be compelled to admit that all our mathematical calculations for centuries past are nothing but fictions, and the discoveries of Newton mere coincidences. I had followed up this shot by pointing out the fact, "that the theory would encourage justice, enlarge our sympathies and promote charity far beyond anything that Christianity had done in this direction." That was what was troubling me now. I, too, had had my sympathies aroused by the extreme poverty of this family, and my generosity appealed to by their dire necessities, but I had done nothing for humanity's sake, while Mel, the Christian, had. It seemed a practical refutation of my argument. I could not explain it satisfactorily to myself, but my faith in the theory was in no wise weakened.

That night after retiring I thought long and seriously of the disadvantages that I must labor under should I become a contestant for Rose's love. Owing to my extreme diffidence I had as yet passed scarcely a word with her, and I was conscious that as compared with Mel's address and self-possession this very diffidence would be the greatest obstacle to my success. Mel also had the advantage of me in personal appearance. Physically he was greatly my superior, financially even more so. He had already won renown and a fair competence in his chosen profession, while I at that very moment was hopelessly stranded — wrecked by a Kansas boom, and the groan which Mel had checked in my store a few days before vented itself with redoubled force from its long suppression. My cousin came hurrying in from an adjoining room to see if I was suffering from heart disease or an epileptic fit. I pleaded the nightmare and was left to my dismal reflections, which finally culminated in the thought that my case was altogether hopeless. Having promptly decided that it was utterly impossible for me to win the prize, I experienced great relief and soon forgot my disappointment in sleep.

In the morning I awoke, feeling vaguely conscious of having come through a painful ordeal, but it was several minutes before I remembered that my trouble was a disappointment in love. I laughed at it now, but, absurd as it may seem, it had cost me a sharp struggle to give up all hope of winning Rose Pardee. For the remainder of our stay I avoided the young lady as much as possible, and no one, I was sure, even suspected my secret. I enjoyed the visit notwithstanding that I must daily witness the progress Mel was making, which but for the fact that I had completely throttled my own hopes would have embittered these days beyond endurance. As it was I was beginning to look forward with pleasure to gaining such a sweet cousin as Rose. Mel's kindness in making the little gift years before, and her appreciation and grateful remembrance of it, did more to ripen their friendship than years of ordinary acquaintance would have done.

Pete did not put in an appearance until the third day after our arrival, as Mr. Lesage had not expected us so soon. Pete was to return at once if any of us had arrived, and so desired, or he was to wait for the others, just as we preferred. We concluded to wait, and two days later the students joined us. Pete was rather cool in his reception of the new arrivals, and we ourselves had fared no better, as he had omitted in both instances the hearty handshake we had naturally expected. Otherwise he was the amiable old darkey he had ever been.

The students, or rather ministers, wished to visit with the Pardees for two days in order to rest after their long journey, and as we had the time to spare we all agreed to it. Pete, however, had grown homesick, and it required all of Mel's persuasive powers to prevail on him to grant the extension of time.

Our visit altogether was a most pleasant one. There were saddle-horses, a carriage and spring wagon, with good roadsters to draw them, at our service. We indulged in a picnic every day or so, while excursions to some point of interest were an every-day occurrence. For the day preceding our departure to the "Mountain Retreat" Rose had planned a picnic in which many of the neighboring ranchmen's families participated. It turned out to be a visit to the Lovers' Pool. We were unaware of our destination until we found ourselves in the cañon which we remembered so well from our scare over Mel's fall into the pool. Rose had appointed Bub, who had taken a holiday, to tell the sad story of the lovers who had drowned themselves in the dark pool. By some chance we had never mentioned the fact that we were already acquainted with the tragedy, and knew a sequel to it that would be a pleasant surprise to our mountaineer friends, when they heard it. When Bub had proceeded far enough to indicate that it was the story of Mose and Jennie he had undertaken to relate, Mel interrupted him and told the more interesting story of the lovers' escape. The discovery that Mose and Jennie were in all probability alive created a perfect tempest of excitement. We had to pilot the party to the crevice and thence to the grotto before we could convince them of the possibility of their friends' escape. That 28th day of July, 1889, was an eventful one to the mountaineers, and the revelations to which it gave rise formed the theme of an amount of delightful talk that it would be useless to try to estimate. About three years previous to that time the Andrews ranch had begun to undergo a great transformation. The place was a fine one to start with, and it had been improved and beautified in numerous ways. A splendid house was in course of construction at that time, and yet no one in the neighborhood knew who owned the place. Our friends of the picnic at once surmised that Skein had bought the place, and was fixing it up preparatory to making it his permanent residence. The fact that the two had never made their whereabouts known, or even intimated that they were alive, could only be accounted for on the ground that they supposed that all their old friends had mistrusted Mose wrongly, and hence had determined to ignore them for the future. We returned home late in the afternoon, after what we voted the most enjoyable day of the season.

The next morning we were making preparations to

accompany Pete up the mountain. It was arranged that we were to make several visits to the Pardees during our two months' vacation. That Mel was the prime mover in planning the visits did not surprise us. Preparatory to starting we all refreshed ourselves with a good drink from the spring. While the others lingered talking with Bub and filling a keg with spring water to be taken with us, I walked around to the front of the house, on my way to the big wagon, which stood about one hundred yards down the walk, with Pete in the driver's seat waiting impatiently for us to "tumble in." To my consternation Rose joined me at the veranda steps and accompanied me to the gate, just beyond which stood the wagon. She had seized the last opportunity, as I thought, to have a little chat with the only one of the party with whom she had not in all this time found a chance to converse, the result being that we walked to the gate in profound silence. For the life of me I could not think of anything to say. Every unsuccessful attempt to think of something relevant to the occasion left me more and more embarrassed. At the gate I did venture to look at her, only to be plunged into deeper confusion by the unmistakable merriment that danced in her sparkling black eyes. But her expression changed on the instant to one of seriousness, and with a look that thrilled me through and through she extended her hand to bid me good-bye, saying as she did so, " Your bashfulness, if you do not overcome it, will lose you the woman you love," and with a quick pressure of the hand she was gone, leaving me surprised and bewildered beyond

measure. Pete broke the spell by saying: "Dat Miss
Rose's a pow'ful fine gul, and, Boss, yo' done got de
inside trak or dis chile dunno nuffen about sentiments."
I answered with some remark about the weather, and
in a manner that checked his thoughtless speech. I
trusted that my great reserve would imply that any
further familiarity on that subject would not be
tolerated. Not for the world would I have had him
joke me about Rose when the others were present.
Rose regained the veranda just as the others came
around from the spring. She stood in the door-way
and waved them an adieu with her hand as they filed
down the walk. On seeing this Pete turned around,
saying, as he slapped me good naturedly on the
shoulder, "By golly, Boss, ole Pete's right all de same.
She didn't 'low none of dem other fellers a chance to
squeeze her purty hand. It's a cold day when dis
nigger gits left on sentiments."

"For heaven's sake," I implored, "don't say anything about this when the boys get here."

"Do yo' members," Pete asked, grinning, "when
you tried to skeer me an' make me tink Marse Gaston
gwine to hang me? Spects dis ole coon gwine to get
eben now."

So much for my attempt to assume a cold dignified
manner toward Pete when he first quizzed me. Pete,
so good natured and obliging usually, had succumbed
to the sweets of revenge, and I had no doubt that he
would torture me to his heart's content. Remembering that Pete had also become a convert to the
theory of permutation of personality, I asked him to

bear in mind that he would be in my place some day, and urged that he ought to be merciful.

"Dat's so," he answered with perfect confidence, which no doubt was born of his great faith in his employer rather than of his rational belief in the theory. He fell into a sober meditation, which lasted through the "tumbling in" process, and so worked on his charity that he spared me any further allusion to the episode of the morning.

I, too, soon fell into serious meditation, while Mel grew actually glum. Was Pete mistaken after all? How my heart bounded, even at the supposition that he was not. But for Pete's positiveness in the matter, my diffidence would have prevented me, even at that time, from construing Rose's overture into anything more significant than friendship. Not that I trusted much to Pete's knowledge of "sentiments," but his assertions encouraged me to consider Rose's conduct more carefully, with the result that I finally decided that she must have fallen in love with me, and I began to analyze the process. She had at first, no doubt, been piqued at my total indifference to her society, which I had assumed in self-defense. Then had arisen the desire, very faint at first, for the society which was so persistently withheld, the desire growing as my indifference became more pronounced. Absorbed with the novelty of not being sought after, Mel's attentions had failed to have the influence that by all rights they should have had. I was the object of her interest, and so became the object of her affection. Later, by intuition, she had divined my secret, but had attributed

my persistent avoidance of her to my bashfulness;
then with that frankness characteristic of the family
she had intimated in an unmistakable manner that I
had but to overcome my timidity to win her. My
dreams up to this point had been very bright, but
there I again experienced a sense of disappointment
in Rose. She had undoubtedly been a little bold in
her declaration of a sentiment which I had in no wise
encouraged, however I might have desired it. I found
myself questioning the womanliness of it, and inclined
to censure her for a want of maidenly modesty. Yes,
there was something that artificial culture had not
been able to give. Not many days previous I had
read of an accomplished society belle, who had made
slight advances towards a poor lover whose pride
would not allow him to disclose his passion. A happy
union had resulted, and I had admired the character
of the lady very much, had even wished with a sigh of
regret that there were more ladies who would take
the initiative in these matters. And now that my
wish was granted I was far from being satisfied. I
accounted for my admiration for the society belle
from the fact that she had been portrayed as a highly
accomplished and refined lady. But wherein had Rose
fallen short of the same standard of culture? I had
mentally found fault with her for her hasty solicitation
of autographs, but her motive once understood, there
was nothing that the most exacting could have
criticised. No, Rose had been the perfect gentlewoman
in every respect, while I was a hypercritical churl, and
so far as self-condemnation would make amends for

my criticisms, I made full atonement for my fault. Still I felt that I ought never to have doubted Rose's infinite goodness and refinement. I was over-exacting. It was a species of pettishness, I told myself, arising from my poor health. This made me think of Mel and the robust health that he enjoyed. There was no denying that Rose had shown a sad want of judgment in giving her heart to a fault-finding invalid, instead of to my good natured, healthy, prosperous cousin, who had been so zealous in his wooing. That I should have been the favored one was simply a miracle. It would be a hard blow to Mel when he learned the truth; indeed, he seemed already very much cast down. Probably he had surmised that his love was hopeless. From the bottom of my heart I pitied him, and I said to myself, there is nothing I would not do to help him bear his disappointment. Then why not help him—or rather, why not bear it altogether? Rose's love for me, having originated as it did, could not be deep seated, however true it might be. If I were out of the way there could be no doubt that Mel could yet win Rose. But no, I could not renounce such happiness. It was more than could be expected of mortal man. It was not as if Rose loved Mel and I had some prior claim that she was bound to respect, no matter how disagreeable it might be. In that case any gentleman would relinquish such prior claim. It was the lady's happiness that must always be considered, and in this case Rose's happiness depended on my returning her love. But my self-questioning would not stop at that. Was I truly considering Rose's happiness in accepting the affection she had so generously given? My judgment told me that Mel was far more worthy of her, and that he could make her far happier than I. They were much better suited to each other than Rose and I were. Then there was the welfare and the happiness of possible descendants to be considered. While I was heart-free I had not hesitated to say that marriage for me was out of the question, even criminal. The taint of consumption, which had driven me to Colorado in the first place, had in the lower altitude of Kansas reasserted itself to an extent that made me fully alive to the fearful consequences to others that should inherit the disease. If it was ever a man's duty to renounce a great happiness it was mine. But would I be renouncing a great happiness in giving up Rose to Mel? Certainly not if the theory of permutation of personality was true, as I believed it was. Self-renunciation in this case was an investment guaranteed to yield a handsome return in my own ultimate happiness. I need not think of Mel's pleasure or of Rose's. My own happiness, to put it on a purely selfish basis, would be my reward in trying to make these two happier. The greater happiness that they should enjoy by my present sacrifice would become mine when I, the ultimate atom constituting my personality, should become the personality of the organisms that they now tenanted. Nor was this the only motive presented to my consideration. So surely as I married Rose, embittered lives would follow, and not only our own lives would be wrecked, but that of every creature in existence. Just as I determined now for good or

evil, so would every personality determine when, in
the course of its progress, it came to inhabit this weak
consumptive body of mine. Oh, what a fearful responsibility rested upon me! The fate of untold millions
of souls depended on my will, and again that indefina-
ble conviction of the truth of the theory thrilled
through me that I had experienced on witnessing
Pete's rapture when he contemplated the hope it held
out to him. The realization of the solemn relations
in which it placed me to the universe and my fellow-
man, impelled a belief in its truth. I did not forget
that should I act selfishly in this matter, marry Rose,
and entail upon all existence the bitter consequences,
I would still be doing right. So much misery must be
in the world in any case, and this selfish act would
but contribute an essential element to happiness itself.
But it in no wise weakened the motive for acting
unselfishly, for it remained just as true, that as I now
acted for weal or woe, so must every sentient being
act. It was nothing to my credit that I promptly
decided that Mel should win Rose, so far as I could
contribute to that end. The personality that had
inhabited my organism during the preceding cycle
had also caught a glimpse of the great responsibility
resting on each individual, and had been prompted by
the mighty motive to right doing, to act just as I had,
and there was virtually no other course for me to
follow. The concatenation of events that had revealed
the glimpse of my true relation to mankind and the
universe had so wrought upon us — the personalities
that had successively tenanted my organism — that

we acted in accordance with the demands of morality, in obedience to that "power that makes for righteousness."

But my duty seemed not to be wholly performed in renouncing Rose. She must be saved any unnecessary suffering from the fact that I could not, or would not, return the love that she had lavished upon me. My unconcern, no doubt, had been the one attraction, and I had been so distant since our acquaintance that she had had no opportunity to rightly estimate my faults. She had certainly overestimated my temper and intellectuality. This must all be changed, even if her love must degenerate into aversion. When we again visited the Pardees I should no longer avoid Rose, but my attentions should become an actual persecution. She should learn just what a supercilious, fault-finding, irritable misanthrope I really was. I should even exaggerate my faults if I found it necessary. As to her superstition in regard to my being a companion for her intellectually, I should leave no means untried to convince her of my utter imbecility. No doubt I deemed this a far more difficult task than it really was, for I expended much hard thought in studying out a line of conduct that would impress Rose with my entire want of common sense. If everything else failed I could give her a history of my Kansas speculations, though the employment of such severe measures was fraught with some danger to one unaccustomed to sudden and painful shocks. By the time we stopped for dinner I had grown very confident that my efforts to dispel Rose's infatuation would prove a complete success.

Owing to the improved road, the trip up the mountain was made much more easily and in less time than of old. We arrived at the Retreat a little before noon of the second day after leaving the ranch. Mr. Lesage, looking somewhat older, but serene and content, came out to the wagon to receive us. He greeted us warmly, even affectionately, his face fairly beaming with delight as he held each one's hand in a long friendly clasp. Pete, who had greeted us so coolly at the station, now, by some strange whim, deemed it the proper time to receive us as becoming one who should reflect rather than foreshadow his employer's cordiality, and he also grasped our hands, giving each a hearty shake, expressing himself as "Pow'ful glad to see yo' back and lookin' so peert." As we had been with him almost constantly for a week we were so lost in astonishment that we did not respond so warmly perhaps as his honest heart deserved.

CHAPTER VII.

EVOLUTION AND SENTIMENT.

In the afternoon Mr. Lesage conducted us to the summit of the mountain, where he had set up his second instrument, and built a tasteful and substantial shelter for it and himself. When the cold weather had come on, he had connected the auroraphone with the house by means of wire, and an ordinary battery, so that some one of his household was always within hearing of the instrument. Any further communications from Saturn would be received at the house. An hour was spent viewing the familiar scenes from the summit.

We had expected a message from Saturn on that day, or during the night, but none came. Much to Mr. Lesage's delight I had learned to play chess since our previous visit, and while the others enjoyed themselves hunting and fishing, the old gentleman and I played chess and waited on the auroraphone. We had been enjoying Mr. Lesage's hospitality for three days before Saturn was heard from. A shower had driven the boys into the house, and Mr. Lesage and I were deeply absorbed in our favorite game, when "Earth" was called in the tickings so familiar to us. As Mr. Lesage was on the point of rising to go to the instrument it continued to click and he sat still listening to

the message. Presently he and the telegrapher of our
party exchanged smiles after the aggravating manner
of those who understand something wholly unintelligible to the others present. We were left but a moment
in ignorance, as our host explained that we were told
to continue the game, and that while our correspond-
ent realized the danger to disinterested persons who
interfered in a game of chess, yet in order to show
us how clearly he could see through the optigraph he
asked permission to suggest a few moves for the black
men, trusting to distance to preserve him from harm.
As the black men, which I was playing, were badly
beaten, I readily assented. By following the directions
given by our Saturnian friend I soon checkmated my
opponent.

The game finished, the auroraphone continued:
"We have learned nothing further in regard to Mr.
Bozar, and I see that the copy of his communication
ends with an account of the insurrection of the dummies, which was then just beginning. I suppose that
the revolt occupied his whole attention at the time
and prevented him from continuing his report. I
shall be pleased to take up the story, and continue
the brief history of our people up to the present time.
But first, Daniel Shepard Holmes, the President of
our Nation; Fabian Beauchamp, the Governor of this
State, and E. Harmon Velasquez, the Mayor of
Damarque—the Capital City—send greeting, instruct-
ing me to assure you of their great pleasure at the
prospect of becoming better known to the people of
earth, and further express the hope that our relations

may be of the most friendly character and as enduring as the cycles of the universe. I, John Smith, am also delighted to assure you that our people take great interest in their fellow beings of a younger planet, regarding them with sentiments of sincerest love and good will.

"There is not much to be told concerning the war with the dummies. The revolt was a terrible one, the bloody horrors of which no human tongue can describe. It was matal-hearted, matal-armed demons against helpless children. Only where strong walls protected them were any saved. We had been at peace among ourselves and with other nations so long, that many modern cities were without any defenses at all, and whole cities were massacred in a day. But for this long peace, however, I suppose none of us would have escaped. There had been no actual war since the invention of air ships, and consequently the dummies knew nothing of aerial warfare, as we may call it, or rather they had no mechanical appliances in their make up that enabled them to train their terrible electrical guns against an enemy directly above them. It was fortunate indeed that they were likewise incapable of aiming downward, for had they been, our fortified cities must have been destroyed from above, as they could man and sail air ships as well as ourselves. Such air ships as we had were fitted out with the best guns that the matal fiends had left us, and from an altitude of a few hundred feet we were enabled to sweep whole armies of the dummies out of existence. They, too, would endeavor to arm ships to ascend to a

level with our own, and so be able to return our fire,
but as we could see all their movements their ships
would be destroyed before they could attain an altitude
to do us any harm. As all our messages are trans-
mitted by electrical currents, they could not interfere
with our communicating with all the other fortified
cities on our planet. Thus we were enabled to plan a
simultaneous onslaught all over the world. In a
month from the time that the revolt broke out it
ended—terminated by the destruction or disablement
of every one of the matal monsters. The loss of life
and destruction of property far exceeded that of all the
wars of the past of which history gives us any account.

"Warned of the terrible results of too much idleness,
our government has been reconstructed on the broad
principle of labor, as we may call it. Believing that
industry is the root of all good, the political and
military leaders demanded some form of government
that would oblige every citizen to perform a reasonable
amount of work. Great difficulty was at first experienced to determine on the proper means to accomplish
this. Prior to the invention of the dummy there had
been constant strife between labor and capital. One
of our wisest savants of that period had proposed a
solution of the labor trouble, in a work entitled 'A
Retrospective View.' The theory advocated was the
correct one. It failed to produce immediate results,
because it was a system of justice, offered to a people
dominated almost wholly by the spirit of injustice.
Before our wider knowledge of the universe had resulted
in our present religion of justice, the dummy had

solved the problem of labor, and the theory propounded in 'A Retrospective View' was not needed, and so, for the time being, was forgotten. But after the suppression of the revolt the theory was revived, and the new government constructed according to its principles. All individual enterprises were suppressed, and the nation became the sole employer of labor. The government provides for the education and maintenance of every citizen until the age of twenty-one, when he is enrolled in the national industrial army, each member of which receives equal wages. At forty-five he is mustered out, or rather is to be mustered out, to enter upon the enjoyment of life, still drawing his pay but exempt from labor except in cases of emergency.

" Owing to our religious teachings for many generations past, our people readily adapted themselves to the new form of government, and so far it has been a grand success. Our neighboring nations, with the exception of one, have adopted and made a success of the industrial army system. The exception is the great and powerful republic of Kolumba. The people are commonly known as Gracians, as they also had their inspired teacher, one Gracio. It is a fact to be noted, that while the several nations of our planet have had their great scientists, discoverers, and inventors, none but the religious teachers have been honored with a multitude of followers bearing their names as a mark of love and veneration. This we attribute to the fact that religion ranks above everything in the social and moral growth of nations.

"The Gracians' religion seems to us rather unique. They believe that by the grace of God many are saved for an endless life of happiness beyond the grave, while the unsaved are doomed to endless torment. Many of their foremost teachers have denied that this is the true doctrine of Gracio, claiming that works and man's free will figure largely in the matter of salvation. It seems to our wise men, however, that one of their apostles, Calvanas by name, was the clearest thinker and most logical expounder of the true teachings of Gracio, and he was profoundly convinced that the fate of souls had been predetermined by Deity. It was not, our philosophers said, that Gracio taught the better doctrine of responsibility and free will, but that the spirit of justice impelled his followers to advance beyond the old faiths, while still retaining the name so venerated.

"As a consequence of the doctrine of election in the popular religion, kings were supposed to rule by divine grace. With a more democratic form of government, the rulers were supposed to be somewhat less under divine guidance, but still they were regarded as in some way better than the mass of humanity. Even the possessors of great wealth came to regard themselves as entitled to the worship and service of the rest of mankind, accounting themselves the elect of God, to rule in time as well as in eternity. This kept the gulf between poverty and wealth continually widening, until the dummy came on the scene and bridged over the chasm by doing all the work and lifting every one to a condition of comfort and happiness. For several years prior to the revolt the Gracians had adopted our religion—the belief in the permutation of personality, which, above all religions, insists on the equality of men. But now that they realize the danger of trusting all work to machines, they, too, have determined that people must do the work of the world, to insure safety. But they no sooner determined on this than their old religion was revived with its pernicious doctrine that by grace some of them were not destined to work, while certain others were especially created to serve them. Hence their social and political system is already one of industrial slavery, with its inevitable accompaniments of poverty, suffering, riots, crime and ignorance. It is no wonder that they have revived their old religion, for it serves to justify the rich in their oppressions, and affords in its promises of a blessed hereafter some consolation to the poor wretches that serve them. Contrary to our usual custom we have sent missionaries among them, to try to convert them from the error of their ways, and persuade them again to adopt our system of government, but to no purpose so far. The trouble is that their acceptance of our belief in the first place was but superficial, for they now claim that to inaugurate the industrial system, some of them must sacrifice the remainder of their lives to the good of the succeeding generation—that those who must first enlist in the industrial army are mostly men who are past the age when they should be mustered out, and that to get the system fairly started these must remain in the army until no time is left them to enjoy the fruits of their labor. Thus they even make out the case worse than it is to fortify the old belief. True, we had the same difficulty to contend against, only that our religion, teaching that our old men who must now form the army shall in some future cycle reap the reward of their labors, made it no difficulty at all.

"It may mystify you somewhat that they were not convinced by the demonstrations of Certology. But the reiteration of its theorems brought out the boast that they were descendants of those who had burned wise men for teaching simple astronomical truths which conflicted with the teachings of their sacred books. But still our teachers labor with them, for now we know that the wretchedness and misery which spring from their system must eventually be our own. But we have broad charity for them. Their religion believed in so long cannot be set aside in a day. Our own religion has all along been a preparation for accepting and adapting ourselves to new truths as they are from time to time discovered and recognized. So while we, with perfect faith in the future, are laying the foundation for a grand industrial millennium, they are drifting back into the old condition of class distinctions, corruption, and oppression. Their religion is at the bottom of their trouble. Believing in a God to whom they ascribe every species of injustice, it is only natural that their political system reflects their distorted ideas of deity. Many of their foremost thinkers, who have out-grown the old superstitions, go to the opposite extreme and teach even a more pernicious doctrine, in regard to deity. Dissatisfied with the divine monster of their forefathers, they deny that any such deity exists, and substitute for him the self-existent universe, that goes on sacrificing each generation for the good of succeeding generations, making out of the cosmos a greater monstrosity than the old deity. Here again we have an exact parallel between the conception of deity and the moral and social system growing out of it. These philosophers would have the universe ever progressing, ever assuming new and more advanced forms, but never arriving at a stage of perfection, or a climax where progression must be followed by retrogression. How, from the present cosmical processes, this is possible, they do not care to explain. Then they would have each generation out-stripping the preceding one in morality. They base their hopes of moral progress on the fact that there are many who have lived pure lives and devoted themselves to mankind without any motives drawn from a future life. They disregard the fact that back of these noble lives is an ancestry whose incentive to moral conduct has been their firm belief in future rewards and punishments. These pure lives do but prove that a moral momentum may be acquired, as well as physical momentum. The naturally moral man has acquired a moral momentum that carries him along the moral path without the immediate application of moral force in the shape of religious beliefs. And were men of this type surrounded by a pure moral atmosphere they might live, and transmit to their offspring the power to live perfect moral lives. With social conditions as they are, however, to talk of moral progress without the aid of religious beliefs to appeal to the selfish side of our natures, is as unscientific as to talk of perpetual motion.

"I see by the electrometer that I shall not be able to tax your patience any further at present, and it will be about forty hours"—

The auroraphone ceased, as we supposed from the complete exhaustion of the electrical current, and we concluded that forty hours must elapse before we should hear from Mr. Smith again. Although it was then near midnight we talked for an hour before retiring. Mr. Lesage and myself were the only ones that accepted the Creetans' view of the Cosmos and of the permutation of personality. Mel adhered to his former view, that while the Saturnians had so many doctrines they had yet to learn of the one true doctrine—Salvation in Christ. The students sided with Mel, while Jim held that he was neutral, though he confessed to being somewhat prejudiced against our distant neighbors on account of the destruction of our wonderful orchestra, which he counted a loss far out of proportion to anything we had gained. "Were it not for my prejudice," he said, "I would concede that the permutation of personality was the only process whereby exact justice could be meted out to all. Yes, I will go further," he continued, "and say that if there be an all-powerful deity who controls the operations of the universe, he is certainly guilty of injustice if he don't govern cosmical processes so as to bring about a permutation of personality. I can't see why a great portion of humanity is born diseased and doomed to suffering, unless, indeed, they are bearing a portion of the world's woe, and in that case I think it only justice that I, too, should some time bear the same burden, while they enjoy my good health, bright prospects and clear conscience. It is painful to contemplate all the suffering I must pass through, but others have to bear it, and anything short of making all bear it alike must fall short of justice. Then it is pleasant to contemplate all the pleasure the soul must enjoy in its progress through the various organisms that people the universe. Of course when the soul has made the entire circuit it must start again on the same journey, and so on forever. That is the price of existence. I have been taught that I should go to heaven to enjoy a life of endless happiness, but after all I doubt if that offers as great an attraction as the life of endless activity alternating with pleasure and pain. Even if the idea of heaven be a rational one, I believe there are many men who would choose the life of change though I doubt if the idea of uninterrupted happiness is a rational conception."

Mr. Lesage and I could but be pleased with Jim's neutrality.

One of the students who, two years before, had lost his wife and child, now brought out a phase of the new doctrine which, to him, seemed very objectionable. "This love," he said, "which we have for the companion of life, is it not in cases like my own ever doomed to disappointment? I have nothing to which

to look forward but the two short years of my married
life, to satisfy my hope of meeting again my first and
only love. All the suffering that I must endure can
purchase but those two years of companionship.
What companionship with others can recompense for
that which I have lost? and of all those seasons of
domestic bliss in which I am to participate none can
equal my own had it but been continued to old age."

Here Mr. Lesage answered: "To my mind this
seems the most beautiful part of the theory, as it
forces us out of ourselves. You must look for your
consolation to those same instances of complete companionship continued to the close of life. You are
inclined to think that the companionship of yourself
and wife was superior to all others. In this you err,
for granting that yours was the most perfect love and
the happiest companionship of the present times, yet
future developments must produce happier conditions
and more pleasurable domestic relations, which you
will enjoy all the more keenly when you come to inhabit
the organisms of that period." Not caring to argue
the point, the student remained silent. One of his
companions now expressed himself as greatly puzzled
as to how he could be his own father and mother, as
he must be if the theory were true. But in fact this
could have puzzled him no more than to conceive how
he could be any other person. He was evidently con-
founding personality and the organism, as his personality could act as the personality of his father's or
mother's organism with the same consistency that it
could act as the personality of any other organism.

Mr. Lesage, to whom we looked for explanations of the knotty points, did not deem the objection of sufficient importance to merit any reply from him. Another of the students was skeptical about an ulti-mate atom constituting personality. "Physiology taught that every particle of the body was changed every seven years, so he couldn't see how there could be that exchange of personalities which the theory demanded. Besides, modern psychologists contend that the ego, or personality, is a succession of ideas, —the sum of our conscious states, and this again is inconsistent with the theory of permutation."

Mr. Lesage, in reply to this, assured us that he had made a careful study of these points and that he could find nothing that seemed to be inconsistent with the theory of an exchange of souls. "From a materialistic standpoint," he said, "personality must belong to the organism, or to the ultimate atom which survives all changes of the organism. If the organism changes from time to time, and still transmits the personality to the succeeding organism, so might the ultimate atom personality change and still transmit the per-sonality to the succeeding atom. One is just as reasonable as the other. The point is that a certain ultimate atom, by being in a certain place at a certain time, is responsible for our personality, and granting that it passes away the next moment after originating the personality of the organism, it must, in the ceaseless activity of the cosmos, serve to originate the person-ality of every organism that comes into existence. The succession of conscious states is dependent on an organism, and the real ego must be sought for at the conception of the tiniest organism from which this organism we call the body is derived. So that whether we are an ultimate atom, a group of atoms, a 'bundle of states of consciousness,' a 'succession of peculiarly combined atoms,' a 'faint manifestation of the unknowable' or a 'series of memories,' the permutation of personality follows from a limited active universe.''

The telegrapher said he had been wondering why it was that the Creetan's language having developed just as our own, yet has different names for the planets.

"This,'' Mr. Lesage answered, "I can't explain further than to remind you that it could not have been otherwise. Had their language grown exactly as our own they would have called their planet earth, and would have had to designate our planet by some other name which would involve the same dissimilarity. The names had to differ in regard to the planets, and their nomenclature is, no doubt, the natural one, and just as good as any.''

With these things to ponder over we retired.

The following day Jim and the students devoted to hunting and fishing; Mel wrote letters, while Mr. Lesage and I played chess, and discussed the Creetan philosophy, or the scientific moves which had been suggested by Mr. Smith. Mel seemed to be reasonably cheerful considering his disappointment in love. However, it would not do to allow him to suffer in any degree, when there was no necessity for it. I must manage in some way to encourage and cheer him up with the knowledge that he was to be the successful suitor for Rose's hand. That evening one of the men, who had been sent to the station for supplies, returned, bringing the mail. Mel was the only one of our party that received a letter, which, with an inexplicable twinge of jealousy, I suspected was from Rose. He brightened up perceptibly when the letter was handed to him, but its perusal was followed by such marked despondency that I pitied him more than ever. At first I had thought it hardly proper in Rose to write to Mel and not to me. But it was very womanlike after all. She would feel a delicacy about writing to one who had not yet declared himself, though it was fully understood between us that our love was mutual. Still she would write to her friend without restraint. Yes, I must at once curb the tendency to criticize Rose, for had it not been proved time and again that I was at fault?

Later in the evening Mel started out for a moonlight ramble up the trail that led to the Summit. Not doubting that I should find him in the lodge which had been built to protect the auroraphone, and wishing to cheer and encourage him, I followed my cousin a few minutes later. He evidently wanted to be alone, but as I was going to reverse our positions and become the comforter, I had no hesitancy in intruding on him. As I had expected, I found Mel in the lodge, sitting at the open window gazing at the silvery moon, which sailed calmly and serenely past light fleecy clouds, all unconscious of the pain that throbbed in Mel's aching heart.

"Well, old boy," I said, "you've come up here to have a fit of despondency all to yourself, have you?"

"Yes," he answered, "but you do not seem inclined to allow me any such indulgence; and now that you've come I will just take you into my confidence and make you share my trouble, though you, no doubt, will regard the whole thing as a very trifling affair. My profession, as you know, is far more to me than to most physicians, and I can say without boasting that my removal from the little community where I have been practicing will be regarded as a calamity, so earnestly have I tried to be a friend and healer to my patients. It is only in hopes of extending my sphere of usefulness that I have decided to seek a larger field of action. But when I shall have once settled down to my work in the place I have chosen, it is to be for life without absence or holiday, for where is the physician that can be spared even for a day from the sufferers to whom it is his holy mission and highest pleasure to administer?"

"Well," I responded, "you are surely not begrudging this little respite of two months, are you?

"No, I can't say that I begrudge it, but I believe I regret it. It is like this. I have concluded to marry, and the lady of my choice, I am convinced, loves me devotedly, but positively refuses to entertain the idea of marriage for a year yet."

Feeling that this was indeed a trifling matter, I broke into a hearty laugh, greatly relieved at the thought that Mel had been already engaged before he met Rose, and so had suffered no disappointment in that direction. It seemed to me, then, that if I only had Rose's infatuation for me dispelled I should not have had a care in the world.

"I knew you would make light of it," Mel said, "but you do not realize the seriousness of it yet. After a careful consideration of the subject, I believe I ought to get married during this vacation, even though I extend it two or three months for the wedding trip. If I once get to work with a number of patients needing my daily attention, it will be a sore trial to my conscience to desert them even for so important a matter as matrimony; to leave them for the length of time that I should want to devote to a wedding tour is simply out of the question. I can't well continue this vacation for an entire year, in order that my practice may not interfere with my honeymoon. So you see, cousin, that to a conscientious man like myself, the lady's obstinacy—I can call it nothing less—is a serious matter. It seems to me that if she loves me as devotedly as she pretends, she would see the reasonableness of my demands, and consent to an early marriage. Sweet tempered and sensible as we know her to be in all other respects, you will surely agree with me that in this Rose in unreasonable."

Rose! The long whistle of astonishment to which I gave vent was genuine, if the laugh which I affected was not. Despite my high-minded scheme of renunciation, this discovery created a sensation similar to that created by my tumble into the icy pool of the cavern, though in this case there was no agreeable reaction. No, I felt only a bitter sense of loss, of humiliation and vindictiveness. "Such scandalous affairs, thank fortune," I thought, "are rare. Rose and Mel engaged after an acquaintance of only eight days!" There was boldness for you! Here, indeed, was a taint of the inherent ill-breeding of the Pardee family, coming to the surface. It was some satisfaction to think that I myself had not been duped by the country girl's coquetry, but that Pete, the conceited old idiot, was wholly to blame. So much for Pete's knowledge of sentiments and my own analysis of the feminine heart. Fortunately it was so dark that Mel could not see my face, as it must have shown the rancor and mortification that I felt. I could do nothing more in the capacity of a comforter, and for the next few days I was myself very despondent. It was one thing to voluntarily give up the woman I loved, and quite another to have to give her up. Feeling that my gloom and Mel's perplexity made rather a poor combination for cheerfulness, I excused myself, and, leaving him to his meditations, returned to the house, a madder but wiser man. I was glad when on the following evening Saturn was heard from, as it helped both my cousin and myself to forget our troubles.

"I have just returned," said Mr. Smith through the auroraphone, "from a meeting of philosophers, scientists and statesmen which had been called to discuss the true uses of labor in the economy of the universe. Since all classes have been working there has been such a marked improvement in our people generally that labor is now thought to be the most important factor of progress. A species of culture and refinement may spring up apart from labor, but for the true intellectual development of a people, minds and hands must be trained together. Advancement may be made where all the manual labor falls to one class and all the higher mental work to another class, but where all participate in the labor and all have a chance, and, indeed, are compelled to engage to some extent in intellectual pursuits the progress is much more rapid and satisfactory. Then the question arose, what is the use of intellectual development? From the discussion of these points, to-day, a higher idea of deity has been developed. That intelligence grows not only by the exercise of it, but by inheritance, has long been regarded by us as a truism. In its origin, consciousness was wholly dependent on an external excitant. Given an organism, no consciousness could have arisen without some external object to make an impression on that organism. Hence it is a truth that there can be no consciousness without the antithesis of subject and object. But while it was absolutely necessary for the origin of consciousness that there should be such antithesis, yet by development through inheritance we are becoming less dependent on the objective element of consciousness. This is so evident that many of our most profound philosophers contend that the mind creates the external world, instead of the operations of mind being determined by objective existence. It had been contended by other profound philosophers that an objective cause is necessary to every mental operation. These two factions, to day, reconciled their differences on the principle of inherited predisposition. it was agreed on all hands that intelligence starts with simple sensations caused by external objects, that we are yet largely dependent on such external causes, but that there are processes at work which must result in consciousness altogether independent of an objective cause. That there is no need of this independent consciousness as long as there is subjective and objective existence is made the ground for assuming that such independent consciousness can exist only in the universe as a whole. The cosmos being one, alone, and limited, if conscious at all must be conscious independent of any external cause. This supreme consciousness must itself be developed, and the progress made by each individual, nation, planet, and system of planets, is so much towards the upbuilding of an all-conscious sentient Deity. The past and future are obscure to our relative intelligence, but the gradual evolution of this supreme intelligence is the key to all those problems of a First Cause, of change from absolute to relative life, and the final change, at the close of each cycle, from relative to absolute life. All relative motion must be transformed into absolute motion—that is, all relative motion of the various parts and atoms of the universe must expend itself in producing the one absolute rotation of the whole mass. This mass now rotating in a perfect void must, so far as our relative intelligence can divine, continue its absolute rotation for ever, unless there is developed an intellectual force that controls its action just as there has been developed an intellectual force that has, within limits, or relatively, control of our bodies. This is the supreme function of intelligence, to perpetuate the life and activity of the universe. Universal labor, by promoting universal intelligence, thus becomes the most honorable and sacred duty of man. As the personality of relative beings is dependent on an ultimate atom, so will the supreme personality be dependent on an ultimate atom. It, too, must have made the long round of relative existence before it becomes absolute. It is entitled to remain in absolute existence for a period of time equal to that passed in relative existence, but to remain longer in the absolute condition, though having the power to do so, would be injustice,—a direct violation of the law that action and reaction are equal and opposite. Consequently when justice is accomplished, and having control of the body—the vast universe—the supreme intelligence works the change from absolute motion to relative motion and begins another cycle, which closes with another ultimate atom becoming the supreme Personality, and so on for all eternity. Each of us in turn must become the absolute. And so existence is made up. Were it anything else it would not be existence. Nor is it blasphemous egotism to look forward to becoming even as Deity himself. The round of relative existence that must be passed through, before we attain to the highest condition, is anything but satisfactory to the ego. Were it within the power of any relative ego to dispense with the relative existence in order to forego the absolute it would no doubt be done at some stage of deep misery in our progress. But we are carried along by the infinite processes and must take both good and bad, high and low conditions. We

are, and cannot cease to be, nor escape bearing our
part of the burdens of existence, neither can we avoid,
if we would, receiving our full share of the pleasure.
The one equals the other, this being the highest expression of the equivalence and transformation of
forces. The final act of creation, as we may call the
beginning of relative motion, is determined by pure
love of justice, and mankind must contribute its quota
of this love by acts of justice to one another. It has
long been contended that no rational account of the
universe is possible without assuming an intelligent,
infinitely-just and all-powerful First Cause. It has been
conceded by our atheistic philosophers that a true explanation of the universe does demand such a First
Cause, but the fearful examples of wrong and injustice
witnessed on every hand negatived any evidence in
favor of an all-wise, omnipotent, beneficent Creator ex-
isting at present. But now all are agreed that this
Supreme Being did exist and gave rise to the universe
in its relative condition, that this Creator is being
again evolved by the processes of the active universe,
and that this supreme outcome of all physical and intellectual processes was none the less beneficent and
wise for making pleasure dependent on pain, since there
is no other way that pleasure could have been introduced into the world at all. The supreme justice of
deity is seen in the fact that all alike must partake of
the sorrow and pleasure through the permutation of
personality.

"I have now given you the main features of the discussion, and trust you will carefully think them over

at your leisure. Since the revolt there are so few of us left, comparatively speaking, that I can spare only an hour occasionally from the regular work I must do as a member of the industrial army. I shall have to excuse myself now for a week, and in the mean time I am sure you can employ yourselves profitably in considering the religious and social principles of our people."

After some talk, we retired, not, however, before Mel had arranged that we were to return to the Pardee farm on the morrow.

CHAPTER VIII.

A FORTUNATE ESCAPE.

EARLY on the following morning we left Mr. Lesage to do most of the thinking over the evolution of deity, and under Pete's care started down the mountain. It was natural that Mel, in view of seeing Rose soon, should regain his wonted good humor. I myself had some ground for feeling cheerful. I was relieved from the prodigious task of covering up my intellectual brilliancies. The harrowing details of the Kansas speculations need never be told to overcome Rose's unfortunate attachment for myself. I had forgiven Rose, and held her in as high estimation as ever. Her little affectionate hand-clasp was just cousinly, and prompted by her womanly affection going out to all that was dear to the one she loved. I was glad to know that she had not even suspected my passion for her, and that she had not was evident from the manner of her leave-taking. I had even forgiven Pete for his conceited officiousness in the matter, and, in fact, felt but little worsted by my love affair. If I could only keep my secret, all would be well, and by shunning Rose as I had done before there would be but little danger of anyone suspecting my infatuation.

In due time we arrived at the farm and were cordially received by the Pardees. It soon became evi-

dent, however, that a cloud had fallen on the family
during our absence. The troubled look I had noticed
on Bub's face when he spoke of his father was now
habitual. Rose, too, had lost much of her cheerfulness, while Mr. Pardee and his wife both seemed out of
humor, the former unusually reticent, the latter driving and scolding. Mel and Rose seemed not over
joyful in their reunion. It was evident that the controversy between them in regard to the wedding day
was becoming more and more serious. Our time was
employed much in the same way that it had been
during our former visit. On the fourth day after our
return Bub seemed more troubled than ever. That
day, from our glowing accounts of the lower cave,
Mr. Pardee, and Bub, whose school was now closed,
had been prevailed upon to accompany us on a visit
to the "Conservatory of the Gods." Doubting
whether the ladder which we had left spanning the
"Tourists' Bath" ten years before was still intact,
we constructed another one. With considerable
trouble we conveyed it to the lower end of the slanting passage, only to find our way completely blocked
by a mass of rock and stalactites. We now remembered that one of the results of the bolt of electricity
from Saturn was a fall in the lake of about ten feet. This
body of water rushing down the incline had swept
everything before it, piling the conservatory full of
rubbish. We had hard work now to make Mr. Pardee
and Bub believe that there had ever been any cavern
beyond the passage.

As we returned home Bub and I dropped behind

the others, and he improved the occasion to bring out the family skeleton, and asked my advice as to how it should be dealt with. It appeared that when Bub came home from college about two years previous to this time, he had been installed as book-keeper and financier of the estate, which consisted of the farm, several tenement houses in Denver, some mining stock and money in bank. He of course kept account of all moneys expended and received, giving checks on the Denver National Bank to the members of the family, when they desired funds for their own use. During the hunting days of his poverty, Mr. Pardee had an old crony in the person of another hunter, Cart Doddwright, who lived, or existed, with his family, much as the Pardees did, about two miles down the river. Mr. Pardee, when he made his find, had generously assisted his old comrade for a year or so, when Mrs. Pardee objected, on the ground that Mr. Doddwright was too thriftless to deserve help. By the aid of money Mrs. Pardee had become a paragon of industry and thrift, and had "no kind a use fur a man who hunted all the time with a big family to support." Mr. Pardee, to keep peace in the family, had pledged himself not to give another penny to his old friend. The Doddwrights, however, had begun to prosper from that time, and continued to improve their fortune, a neat house, good stock, and well tilled farm being the most noticeable features of their improved circumstances. Since Bub had been at the head of affairs he had been puzzled at the fact that his father had repeatedly drawn sums of money ranging from two hundred to five thousand dollars, the disposition of which was a complete mystery to him. He was still more perplexed at his father's manner when he applied for checks. He seemed ill at ease, as though he felt guilty of some wrong-doing. Mr. Pardee invariably departed on a bear hunt immediately after cashing the checks, usually at the store at the station. Bub worried over the matter, but was too loyal to meddle with his father's affairs. The day following our departure for the retreat, Bub had accidentally solved the mystery—the money went to pay gambling debts —his father was a gambler. Cards had been a pastime in the Pardee home, but not so much as a pin had ever been staked on the game. Mr. Pardee was especially fond of cards, and his evenings at home were usually spent with the fascinating little pasteboards. They had not dreamed that his infatuation with the game would entice him into gambling until the day Bub had received ocular proof of it. Riding past the Doddwright home a little after dark, he had been surprised to see his father, who had ostensibly gone on a hunt that morning, playing cards with Mr. Doddwright and two other men, both entire strangers to Bub. The four were in an upper chamber, a lamp burning brightly on the table around which they sat. To get the full benefit of the cool night air, the window and blind had been raised, and while he could not hear, Bub had seen everything that took place. His father and one of the strangers were playing against Mr. Doddwright and the other stranger. The latter, he could see, "were getting the best of the game." Pres-

ently the game ended and Mr. Pardee had taken a
large roll of bills, obtained by cashing the check Bub
had given him that morning, and handed it to Mr.
Doddwright. A little later the party strolled out to
the front gate, where Bub could hear them talking.
Just as his father was leaving, Mr. Doddwright had
said to him: "Wall, we won to-night, but perhaps
you'll have better luck next time. Come down Satur-
day night and we'll have 'nother game." Mr. Pardee
had consented and said something about bringing
along a balance of two hundred dollars, which he still
owed Mr. Doddwright. He had then struck out by a
mountain path for home. After the others had returned to the house, Bub had ridden on almost
heart-broken at his discovery. He found his father
at home when he arrived, as the footpath over the
mountain was much the shorter route. Mr. Pardee
had seemed unconcerned, and affected high humor.
Almost immediately after Bub had come into the
room, it being still early in the evening, his father had
bantered him for a game of euchre. Bub for once
had refused, with a show of ill humor, and had made
some demand on Rose that also prevented her from
employing her father in his favorite amusement. Bub
told Rose everything, and from regarding cards as
harmless, they had come to look upon them as extremely dangerous and hurtful. They, at least, would
play no more, and this it was that had driven Mr.
Pardee into such ill-humored silence, for as yet he was
all unconscious of the fact that his children knew of
his vice. Mrs. Pardee had also been made acquainted

with her husband's depravity. On any minor faults
she did not hesitate to lecture as any good woman
should, but the very enormity of this sin made it impossible for her or the others to take the culprit to
task for it.

It was evident to my mind that the two strangers
were sharpers, who, in connection with Mr. Doddwright,
were fleecing Mr. Pardee. I suggested that we at once
take steps to ascertain the truth, and should it prove
as I feared the next step would be to have the "gang
pulled" for confidence men. This would be the quick-
est way to dispose of the parasites who were system-
atically enticing Mr. Pardee to moral and financial
ruin.

That evening was the one appointed for "another
game," and Mr. Pardee had prepared for it by having
Bub write him a check for the two hundred dollars to
be paid on that occasion. Under the circumstances, we
determined to follow Mr. Pardee, and as far as possible keep the party of gamesters under our espionage
for the evening. We could thus determine the character of the men with whom he was playing, and act
accordingly.

It was about the middle of the afternoon when we
reached the house. Mr. Pardee at once declared his
intention "to take a little hunt," adding that "he
would probably be back that night," and with his gun
on his shoulder sallied forth. Bub and I withdrew and
followed our unsuspecting *protégé* with but little
trouble. He first went to the station, probably to
cash the check. He remained there about an hour,

talking with neighbors, who happened to be at the one store of the place for trade or gossip. Just as our patience was beginning to waver, he made his appearance and started down the road leading to Mr. Dodd-wright's. We followed at a safe distance. A walk of a little more than a mile brought us to our destination, about sundown. Bub and I took refuge in a little clump of trees at one side of the road and but a short distance from the grounds. We were too far away to hear any ordinary tones from the house, still we had a good view of the premises. I was surprised at the beauty and order of the place. It even surpassed the Pardee property in the extent and variety of the trees and shrubs which adorned the grounds. In addition to a profusion of ornamental trees and flowering plants, several acres were devoted to small fruit culture, which seemed to be in a high state of cultivation. The house was of picturesque design, well planned and altogether a splendid building. There were a carriage house, barn, and sheds in keeping with the residence. All were new, as they had just been finished a few weeks before. Bub noticed two new features, which had been added since he rode past the place on the night of his sad discovery. One was a clump of trees of about two years' growth, which had been transplanted on the outskirts of the grounds and only a few yards from the grove in which we were concealed; the other was a beautiful fountain, set off with a few pieces of fine statuary. A spring, far up the mountain, fed the fountain, the waters of which were now sparkling in the yellow rays of the setting sun. For the first time Bub viewed these beauties with anger glowing in his dark eyes. The realization that this magnificence was purchased with money which the wily old hunter had treacherously obtained from his father was not the sole cause of his ire, nor that which made him shake his clenched hand at the three confederates, who sat on the veranda, lazily smoking cigars. He counted it at the cost of his father's honor and manhood, and it was evident that the righteously indignant son would not hesitate to wreak bodily vengeance on the offenders if the law failed to avenge his father's wrongs. A strange foreboding seized me, and there came to my mind a picture of this splendid young man just entering the golden portal of manhood, himself in the clutches of the law, his hands dyed with the blood of his fellow-man. Something prompted me to flee from the spot, and at all hazards to take Bub with me. I yielded to the impulse and begged and entreated him to return home at once. I even exerted my puny strength to drag him from the spot, but all in vain. There was nothing to do but to stay, and with a strange dread at my heart I yielded to the inevitable.

Mr. Pardee had been received at the house with a great show of cordiality by the three men, and after a few minutes' conversation, Mr. Doddwright locked arms with him in a very affectionate manner and the two strolled out into the grounds. Bub's face grew white with rage at this act of fawning treachery. The two old cronies first inspected the fountain and then came down to the clump of trees which had lately been added to the miniature forest. They halted quite near us and contemplated the trees.

"That's 'erbout the way to 'range them," the old fox was saying to his victim. "Got things in purty gran' style I calls it. A little better'n some others in the neighborhood, eh?" and he chuckled with unmistakable gloating and triumph. A sharp clicking sound broke the stillness, and I looked around to see Bub raising a cocked revolver pointing directly at the elated Doddwright. Just at that instant Mr. Pardee stepped between Bub and his intended victim.

"Yes," Mr. Pardee answered, standing so as to shield his companion from harm, "you're a trump, Cart, you just air an' no mistake. I never could get along without you, ole pard. Wife thought you was no 'count, and wouldn't work and got offish and set agin you. But you didn't have nothin' to work with, and it takes money to get us out of the ole ruts that poverty chucks us inter. You've just amazed me since you got ter goin'. I mus' say that you and your ole woman just knock the spots off of Betsy herself, and that's puttin' it hard. It's been a pile of trouble, but it's worth it all and more too. Youngsters think if they've got plenty of 'mon' they can get a place made to order just to suit 'em, and I spoze they can sometimes. But I sot about years ago to fix up places that would persuade the children to stay near me and the ole woman, and I do believe we've done it. Bub'l be gittin' married soon, and won't this just make him a dandy weddin' present? I wish I could tote it in, house, trees, fountain and all, and set 'em down on the center table. It would just everlastingly squash the other presents, wouldn't it? Then I'd make 'em a presenting speech. I'd say, 'Young man, you've got too hifalutin to play keerds with yer ignorant ole pap, but, bless yer soul, I ain't been too proud to look arter yer interests, and here's a place what you couldn't produce its ekal in ten years. There's strawberries and blackberries and everything else that can be made to grow in this climate. You can go into that cute little barn there and milk that darlin' little Jersey cow and just live on strawberries and cream, and honeymoon till you get tired.' It would surprise 'em, it shurely would. No one knows as this is my place. I ain't even had the deed recorded, for fear it would leak out. You could just do me up big if you was a mind to, and I couldn't kick much if you did. You've done all the hard work and managin' and I've just put up the 'mon,' which come as easy as nothin', and then you've looked arter the Andrews place that's to be Rose's weddin' present."

"Yes, and I'll tell you what's the matter," broke in Mr. Doddwright. "Rose and Bub must both get married to once, and at your house, one of them double weddins' we've hearn about. And when all the people are congregated and wondering where's the bride's Honorable Pap and his Gran' Vizer, that's me, here we'll come, me a packing Rose's place, and you a packing Bub's, with the houses and trees, and barns and cows and all, and a big Newfoundland dog like Rose likes a layin' on a rich rug on her porch, and a setter, that Bub likes, a settin' on his porch. In we'll

14

walk a totin' our splendiferous presents, and every-body will say, oh! and the children will clap their hands, and the dogs will begin to bark and both cows will bawl like everything, and such another swell weddin' never will be heard of." Here they both laughed heartily at the conceit, and started back to the house."

And now Bub applied his "golden-portaled" man-hood to the task of dragging me from the spot, with the result that I was carried some distance up the road over which we had lately come. His emotions can better be imagined than told. He had wronged his father in thought, and had almost meanly spied out his most carefully guarded secret. Instead of go-ing to pay gambling debts, the sums of money which had so worried Bub were being carefully expended for his own benefit. It had, no doubt, been the purchase money for the fountain that Mr. Pardee had given to his old friend at the close of a social game of cards, in which the two arch plotters often indulged. Bub's remorse was keen as he thought of his own suspicions, and that he had even persuaded Rose and his mother to share them. The tears streamed from the big fel-low's eyes as he bitterly accused himself of ingratitude and meddlesomeness. My sympathy, however, was with the two old cronies, and I was still laughing at the picture of the unique wedding that was brewing, and hoping that it would be my good fortune to be present when the father and his Grand Vizier brought in the two sections of mountain land and the appur-tenances thereunto belonging, and deposited them on

the center table. But I soon sobered up at the thought
of how near to murder we had been. But for Mr.
Pardee's fortunate change of position, that calm summer day would have ended in a terrible tragedy. Was
it by accident that the timely step was taken? Surely
not, in a universe governed by law. Nor could it have
been providential. Providence had not stepped in to
save hundreds of other innocent victims who had been
killed through mistake. It was strange to think that
in the remote past matter so arranged itself that
through a chain of cause and effect extending through
millions of years, and over a mighty expanse, the exact amount of force was directed to that exact spot
and impelled Mr. Pardee to take that fortunate step—
a force manifesting itself in the imperceptible motive
that influenced his action. And so, I thought, are all
actions determined by natural forces manifested as the
stronger motive that impels us to act. It was determined millions of years ago, by some little swirl of
atoms, just how we shall act from moment to moment.
How, then, could I attach any moral quality to conduct? Mr. Pardee's step was of that class of occurrences which are termed accidents, and I could not call
it good or bad. At bottom, Bub had no desire to kill
Mr. Doddwright, and, except for a chain of accidents,
would never have been prompted to, and yet, but for
that one step, his unerring aim would have made him
a murderer. We should call it murder in either case,
as the intent was to kill. But the facts would become known, and yet Bub would not be arrested and
arraigned for murder. No, the world would say, prac-

tically, that it was accidental, and not hold him responsible. Had he killed Mr. Doddwright, it would have been no less accidental, and yet the world would now hold Bub responsible, and demand the forfeit of his life. And what if the world does demand the life of the murderer? It is a poor rule that will not work both ways. If all actions are predetermined, then that act whereby society executes the criminal is also predetermined, and no one can find fault with it. It is by setting up a principle and carrying it only half out that the confusion arises about free will and necessity. Those peculiar motions of matter which occurred so long ago, giving rise to motives, are the safeguards of society to-day. The antecedents of hunger are, no doubt, traceable to the beginning of the present cycle, and hunger itself, perhaps, supplies stronger motives to action than all else besides. Shall I sit down then and say, " that as everything is predetermined I need not try to get anything to eat; it will be just so anyway." My half allegiance to the principle makes the trouble. It is more pleasant and practical to accept the principle in full, and to perceive that it is equally predetermined that I shall make the necessary exertions to procure food and enjoy it. Society says that people are governed by motives, and forthwith begins to create motives by promises of protection in right doing, and threats of punishment for wrong doing. It was determined ages ago that society should create these very motives, and that they should operate to prevent crime and encourage virtue. The doomed criminal may hold out his manacled hands and implore

mercy on the ground that he is governed by iron law,
is therefore irresponsible, and could not have avoided
doing the crime for which his life is demanded as the penalty. The culprit is willing to admit the principle only
so long as it serves his purpose. Society does but
carry out the man's logic to its legitimate results when
it says, "neither can we help what we are doing," and
springs the drop. Society is governed by the stronger
motive, that of protection, and acts of necessity in
disposing of the murderer. It has the end of self-protection in view, and puts the criminal out of the way
to secure that end. But is this self-protection? Does
it secure the end in view? When we think, that in
hurling the criminal into eternity we are actually hurling ourselves, eventually, into the same place, we may
question whether capital punishment serves the purpose for which it is intended. By the permutation of
personality we must all stand in the criminal's shoes at
some period of our existence. Protection, for the time
being, might be secured by the prompt execution of
the wrong doer, but we bring upon ourselves a more
terrible fate than that which we feared at the hands of
the criminal classes. Bub's object in raising his revolver was to mete out punishment, but had he carried out his intent, how much greater punishment he
would have brought upon himself, and others! It was
his duty to have remembered that the proper way to
inflict punishment in this case was through the law.
What a protection to himself was the law at that time,
had his respect for it been the stronger motive! And
perhaps there is a better, a more humane, a far more

effective method to protect society from criminals than
that of capital punishment. Regard for our future
welfare may constitute a stronger motive than the desire for immediate protection, and lead us to the discovery of some more thorough means of protection.
We may find that society, like Bub, is mistaken, and
that its own defects of constitution give rise to that
criminal class from which it is at any moment liable
to suffer. Perhaps a grand industrial army like that
of the people of Saturn, based as it is on justice
and equality, would afford far better protection than
the most rigorous penal code.

Lost in reflection, we walked back to the farm in
silence. Bub lost no time in placing his father right
with his mother and Rose, though he was careful not
to reveal his secret. Mr. Pardee evidently had the
welfare of his "old pard" at heart in his schemes, and
employing Mr. Doddwright to work and manage the
two places, intended for his children, he deemed no
breach of confidence. He was only helping his old
friend to help himself, and Mr. Doddwright had labored
hard and faithfully, as much for friendship's sake as for
the liberal wages he received.

Mr. Pardee returned early in the evening, and the
domestic and social atmosphere resumed its wonted
temperature. Jim was in no wise prejudiced against
cards, and he and Rose soon had Bub and Mr. Pardee,
greatly to the delight of the latter, pitted against them
in a game of "High-five." Mel, who was opposed to
cards, and I, who was opposed to Rose, did not play.
That night, leaving the students deep in a polemical

discussion, my cousin and I betook ourselves for a stroll on the veranda, and arm in arm engaged in a good natured criticism of each other's foibles. I took him to task for his absurdly high sense of obligation to his patients, and he replied that I held more absurd ideas about marriage. "In making a celibate of yourself," he said, "for fear of transmitting disease, you are downright foolish. Yours is not hereditary consumption, and in the pure, bracing atmosphere of the mountains it is not consumption at all. You would have been a well man to-day if you had remained in Colorado instead of going to a lower altitude. Such recklessness ought to bring you to your present condition."

"You are certainly as careless of your own health," I answered, "in settling down to the hard, incessant drudgery which you contemplate, and which bids fair to interfere very seriously with your matrimonial prospects. Your punctilious regard for the rights of your patients will make a celibate of you yet. The close attention to business which you propose will surely undermine your health and cut short your usefulness. All work and no play will result no better now than in the past. Take my advice and get your practice nicely established, and at the end of the year take a vacation of a few months, get married and enjoy your wedding trip like a rational man. No reasonable patient could object to his doctor going away on a wedding tour even if he died through his absence. Marriage must necessarily take precedence over death any way, and you and Rose will be much happier if you will take a common sense view of the matter and act accordingly. Granting that my views of marriage, as it concerns myself, are as absurd as yours in regard to a physician's obligations, still there is nothing at stake in my case, while your own and Rose's happiness may be wrecked forever if you persist in your high-pressure sense of duty."

It nettled me somewhat to think that these two could not be reasonable, and for once make the course of true love run smoothly. According to my views, it would save every being in existence a great deal of unnecessary trouble and pain if they would compromise the matter some way, and begin to enjoy the sweets of what should be a very enjoyable courtship. My theory of existence made me personally interested in the happiness of these two, and I felt justified in trying to forward it to the extent of offering good advice at least. I felt that my cousin was more to blame than Rose. I could but respect her for not wanting to rush into matrimony with the precipitancy that Mel demanded, and yet it seemed that she ought to acquiesce in his wishes, considering the high motives that gave rise to them. At heart, I did respect Mel's motives, and yet I thought he might lower their standard a little, without hurt to himself or others.

We had subsided into silence, though we continued our walk. I was thinking that I ought not to be worrying over their troubles—that I had plenty of my own to employ myself, if I must worry. I almost regretted having made this last visit. My unhappy passion for Rose was much harder to subdue by my being thrown daily into her society. True, we never conversed with each other, but even the sight of her made it more difficult to keep her out of mind. On our return to the retreat, I for one should remain there until we were ready to depart for home—for Kansas, bright, sunny Kansas. With all its drawbacks of drouths, sand storms, hot winds, and booms, Kansas had a warm place in my heart. There I had seen more bright, sunshiny days, more pleasant summers and milder winters, than anywhere else it had been my lot to live, and I had experimented with the climate of every state north of the 36th parallel, from the Atlantic coast to the Rocky Mountains. I was not homesick, but I should have been content to start for the Sunflower State at any moment.

Mel and I had been walking up and down the long veranda for some time in silence. Presently the game of cards ended, and Rose began to sing and play, and we joined those inside. Rose confined herself to the songs and pieces that her father preferred. This, after cards, was the most effective way to make amends for her unjust suspicions of the past week. Just before parting for the night, Bub had asked his father about the two strangers who were visiting Mr. Doddwright, and learned that they were cousins of the latter, and good honest farmers from Dakota.

But while the social atmosphere had resumed its normal condition, all was not clear yet. My lecture to Mel had had no apparent effect, and he and Rose, to judge from appearances, were no nearer a settlement of their differences. The day before the one set for our departure for the Retreat, I was out with Bub prospecting for a spring that might be made to feed a fountain on the home grounds, as he had become ambitious of outdoing "some others in the neighborhood" in that line. We had been successful in our search, and were returning late in the day. When near home we had met Mel, strolling about looking vexed and morose. A little farther on we had come upon Rose, seated in an arbor, which had developed from the children's first play-house to a cool and elegant structure of rustic design. It was an inviting retreat, where the two grown-up children invariably betook themselves on hot summer days to read or write. Rose, however, was neither reading nor writing, but crying. We hurried past, hoping to give the impression that we had not seen her. When at a safe distance, Bub explained that Rose was still grieving over their unjust suspicions of their father. Perhaps Bub thought that he had divined the cause of Rose's trouble, but I knew that her tears were but the obverse of Mel's gloom and depression.

Arrived at the house, we found Pete on hand with the big wagon, to take us to the Retreat next day.

CHAPTER IX.

MORNING in the mountains. Deliciously cool and exhilarating was the atmosphere, as the orb of day—ancient God of the Creetans—shot his golden barbs over the snowy range, gilding its sinuous crest until it glistened like a great fiery serpent—a monster demon, waiting to contest the rights of deityship with the coming Sun-God. From an open window, looking out through a gap in the mountains to the distant scene of conflict, I watched the struggle. As the blazing champion of light reared himself to hurl his gleaming darts more directly into the huge dragon, the latter twined itself along past diaphanous clouds of vapor, which it exhaled in its writhings. Gaining advantage by ascent, the radiant God showered his burning shafts upon the struggling monster, driving it to the south, so enveloped in its own exhalations that only now and then its burnished scales emitted malignant flashes of light. The opalescent mists proved to be its winding sheet. Gently the south wind turned back the silvery shroud, disclosing the dead monster, cold and white, reclining in tortuous curves on its vast *catafalco*, its lurid fires regenerated into dazzling purity by the conquering God. The wind soughing through the trees chanted a requiem for the dead; the soft air fragrant with the breath of pines and the perfume of flowers, sent up grateful incense to the victorious Deity, while hundreds of sweet-throated warblers sang his praise.

An hour later, I had again preceded my comrades to the big wagon, though Rose had not accompanied me to the gate, as before. It was Mel she shook hands with, and so friendly was their parting, that the observant Pete had no boasts to make about his knowledge of sentiments.

Our trip up the mountain was accomplished without incident. Mr. Lesage was so pleased to see us, so warm in his greeting, that it occurred to me that we were not showing him the consideration which we should, in "packing off" to the Pardees so much. His entertainment was all that we could ask. He it was who had invited us to partake of his hospitality, while we were enjoying the mountain air and scenery. I, at least, should prove more grateful in the future, and do all within my power to cheer and interest this lonely old man, so mild and sweet tempered. My *penchant* for chess was my best qualification for contributing to our kind host's enjoyment. It was but seldom that I won a game, and my victories were hard earned unless, indeed, I received help from Mr. Smith, our Saturnian friend. We voted Mr. Smith a jolly good fellow, and without any good reason, liked him better than poor Mr. Bozar, whom the dummies, no doubt, had as completely pulverized as he had pulverized our orchestra. If we felt a little jubilant over this, we checked the emotion in its incipient stage; for could not the people of Saturn read our very thoughts, and what might we not bring down on ourselves by such uncharitable feelings?

Mr. Smith proved himself worthy of our good opinions. On the first evening after our arrival he hailed us through the auroraphone, stating that the people of Saturn were having a great jubilee over the fact that they had that day established plano-electrophonic communications with Neptune, this being the first interchange of intelligence between the two grand planets. One feature of the celebration was a grand display of electrical fireworks, and Mr. Smith proposed to entertain us a while with a sample of their art by means of the electrical currents. At this we all arose precipitately to object. We had sampled their electricity once before, and had no desire to repeat the experience. We were told, however, by the considerate Mr. Smith to direct our attention to a point about a mile distant, and then for twenty minutes the whole world seemed turned into a pyrotechnical display. We were then told to call for the reproduction of any phenomenon that we wished to see, as from the fact that every earthly event of importance had been noted, and by means of their wonderful instruments, preserved for future reproduction, much on the same plan that our phonograph reproduces sounds. They had but to move the index hand of the Electro-Camera-Lucida-Motophone, so that it pointed to the name of the event to be reproduced, then turn a crank, and the scene appeared at any point they designated, this being done by other adjustments.

We first asked to see the destruction of Pompeii,

with but little confidence in the result, notwithstanding all that we had seen and heard. Ten minutes later there lay before us mighty Vesuvius, the country surrounding, and the beautiful city, peacefully nestling in vine-clad hills, all unconscious of its approaching doom. We were no longer incredulous, and we realized that we were about to witness a scene of terror and suffering, in which we ourselves must eventually participate. The first indication of the eruption was a trembling of the ground on which we stood, followed by a swaying motion, accompanied by low deep grumblings like distant thunder. The waters of the bay heaved and surged as if stirred by some monster leviathan of the deep, while the silvery waters of the river Sarnus tossed about, evidently to the consternation of many boatmen, who were rowing their crafts on the troubled stream. Suddenly a great volume of smoke and lurid flames were belched forth from the volcano. Dazzling flashes of lightning pierced the inky mass, and terrific peals of thunder added to the horrors of the appalling, yet grand scene. We had just time to see the confusion and terror of the people, when the cloud of smoke and ashes settled over the doomed city. A moment later the scene disappeared.

Mr. Lesage now auroraphoned Mr. Smith for the Chicago fire. In due time a great black cloud appeared. From out the dense blackness myriads of lights twinkled and glowed. One of these lights seemed brighter than the others, and grew in intensity, finally revealing the interior of a shed, in which stood a cow, hungrily munching a bran mash. The light proceeded from a

lantern which stood on the ground a little to the rear
of the cow. A woman was milking the docile animal,
which, however, as soon as the mash was devoured,
struck out with her right hind leg, kicking the lantern
over, which ignited the straw that littered the floor.
The flames spread with incredible speed, and in a moment the whole city seemed in flames. The people and
firemen with engines moved about in a confused mass,
while a babel of indistinguishable sounds reached our
ears. The man in Saturn, no doubt, was turning the
crank of the "'phone" with all his might, and so developed the fire much more rapidly than it actually occurred. The flames lit up the city, revealing all the
horrors of that dire calamity, and we stood dismayed
at the terrible experiences through which we ourselves
were destined to pass. But these people before us had
to suffer it, and why not we? Owing to the energy of
the man at the crank the whole scene was turned out in
fifteen minutes, and the fire subdued. At Jim's request
the Battle of Gettysburg followed the fire. It was all
the more striking from the rapidity with which the engagement progressed. Couriers rode to and fro at a
tremendous gait. Infantry rushed at each other with
indescribable fury. Batteries galloped to the front as
if shot from a catapult. Cavalry charged with frightful velocity, and stopped so abruptly that by all the
laws of dynamics the riders should have been precipitated miles to the rear of the enemy. Cannon thun-
dered, shells shrieked, artillery roared, all with such
mad desperation and terrific haste, that within twenty-
three minutes the Confederates were retreating back to

Virginia, and the "backbone of the rebellion was broken." It was evident that the man at the crank did not propose to have any "monkeying" while the Union was in danger.

Satiated with these harrowing scenes we called for something that would show the pleasant side of life, and instead of any grand spectacle, as we expected, there passed before our view a succession of minor events, in which smiling faces, kindly deeds, cheerful words, friendly hand-shakes, children at play, sparkling streams and pleasant groves, were the principal features.

Our distant friend now explained that his assistant at the crank had been so anxious to get away to join in the festivities of the celebration, that he had excused him, and that there would be no further displays that evening. Giving three lusty cheers for Mr. Smith, of Saturn, which we hoped he might hear, we tendered him a vote of thanks, by auroraphone, for the splendid entertainment, and asked for further information in regard to the people of Neptune.

"There is not much," he responded, "that can be of interest to the people of earth, though much that is of great importance to ourselves." We were rejoiced to learn that their government is similar to our own, founded on the grand industrial army system, which grows better by long usage. Founded as it is on justice and equality, it can never wear out. For thousands of years it has brought them universal prosperity and peace, and the highest enjoyment of life. It is no longer a matter of experiment with them, but a grand

and glorious success. The evolution of deity is the solution of the mystery of existence, as tested by their superior advantages of knowing. The permutation of personality has been so long a matter of knowledge with them, and is in every way so consistent with religion and morality, so self-evidently the result of the conservation and equivalence of forces, that it is a matter of great difficulty to make them believe that there are yet intelligent civilized beings who doubt it.

"We ourselves have seen in the evolution of the Cosmos the process of deity-creation. We have recognized that the minute organisms, contributing little by little to higher organisms until man is reached, have been carrying on this process. Through the organization of men into nations, the process is carried still further, history being the vehicle for the transmission of organized experience of a national character. The organization of all nations into one great nation, such as has been consummated in Neptune, by furnishing richer experiences to transmit, furthers the process. And now, the Neptunians speak of a confederation of planets, which becomes possible by means of interplanetary communications, and which will contribute in a still greater degree to the main process. No doubt that out of these world-relations many wars will result, and great battles be fought by contending planets. Thus a wonderful stimulus and expansion will be given to intellectual activity, in planning offensive and defensive operations, in forming interplanetary laws, and in devising great planetary fairs to which innumerable worlds shall contribute, and so another advance be

15

made toward the final cosmical intelligence. The Neptunians also find it difficult to believe that there are those who, knowing that intelligence has been evolved, yet believe it stops with man, and are unable to see that just as the embryonic processes go on to the development of the full-orbed intelligence of the man, so must the cosmical processes go on to the development of the cosmical intelligence."

Jim, who had not been thinking of these last thoughts, now wanted Mr. Lesage to ask Mr. Smith how it was that the sun, which must be no more than a star, to them should be counted a god, and how it was that they could exist in such a hot region as Saturn was known to be.

"The latter," Mr. Smith answered, "is merely a matter of adaptation. Our ancient scientists had it figured out that owing to the extreme coldness of your own atmosphere no life was possible on your globe. So you see that these things must be taken as they are, and not as they should be. The light of the sun, as you are well aware, is largely dependent on the atmosphere. At mid-day, the sun appears for a few minutes no larger than a star, but its resplendence, undoubtedly, is much greater, even at that time, than it is at any time to the people of the earth. This is owing to the great luminosity of our atmosphere. Again, owing to the great height of our atmosphere, and the consequent great refraction of the rays of light, the sun as soon as it passes the meridian begins to grow larger in appearance, and in a few minutes looks much larger to us than it does to you. It is by the refraction of the rays of light that the sun appears larger at the horizon than at the zenith of your own globe. It is also through the refraction of the rays of light by the atmosphere that you see the sun fifteen minutes before it rises and for the same time after it sets. Our atmosphere being so high, it is only during the shortest days of winter that we have any night at all. During the most of the summer it does not get dark before the sun again appears in the east. During the longest summer days we have the sun rising in the east before it sets in the west. Apparently we see the sun both in the east and west, a little above the horizon. Of course its true position is antipodal to that which the beholder occupies during the singular phenomenon. Such unusual refraction requires a high atmosphere, a very high atmosphere."

After expressing a willingness to give us exhibitions similar to the one we had witnessed, whenever we desired them, and informing us that by the success of their improved generators of electricity, they were no longer dependent on natural currents, Mr. Smith excused himself also on the plea of wanting to join in the rejoicings of the occasion.

The following day it occurred to us that Mr. Smith might be able to clear away the mass of stones that barred the entrance to the cavern, by directing a current of electricity against it. We ventured to call Smith and make known our wishes. He responded promptly, expressing his willingness to place himself and the nation's electricity at our service. He had served his term as a common laborer in the industrial

army, and had just been promoted to the position
of superintendent of the electro-planetary station, and
he could now devote the most of his time to us. "Any
work," he said, "which you can give me will be appreciated, as it enables me to contribute my quota to the
world's work in a manner most agreeable to myself.
We are not so pressed for laborers as in the past, as
we are again manufacturing and using many new and
improved labor-saving inventions, but we draw the
line at dummies."

We pointed out the place where the rock lay, and
without any jar or disturbance, Smith soon had the
mass at a glowing white heat, under which it quickly
crumbled to dust. Then came a puff and it all disappeared in a cloud of fine sand, borne away towards
the great sand dunes of the San Luis Valley. An hour
later, we were exploring the cavern and to our great
joy we found that the opening through which the water
flowed into the orchestra had been dammed up by the
debris on the first wave of the flood. The water being
thus turned down the old bed of the stream the orchestra was saved. We returned to the house, procured
crowbars and picks, and began a vigorous assault on
the rock and poles that obstructed the passage. We
had made but a few strokes, however, when we felt
slight electrical shocks, which we immediately divined
were the observant Smith's mode of admonishing us
to get out of the way and he would do the work. We
hurriedly quit the spot, and Smith proceeded to disin-
tegrate the mass and a portion of the roof of the
cavern. As they crumbled away the particles fell into

the brook, with hissing sounds and little puffs of steam, and were carried off by the current. As the water gradually flowed into the orchestra chamber the music swelled from low soft strains to the full grand harmonies of old. Our happiness was complete. Our next step, however, was to add to it. We returned to the outer world, ascended to the hole made by the electrical current through the roof of the cave, and marked out a half circle by setting up stones a few feet apart. The space so described contained about an acre, and overlooked the valley to the east. On returning to the house we auroraphoned Smith to clear out that part of the mountain described by the stones to a level with the stream which flowed through the cavern, explaining that we wanted the excavation as an audience chamber from which to witness the exhibitions he had so kindly promised us, and at the same time be enabled to enjoy the music of the orchestra. We also described the orchestra, and asked him to throw the scenes in the valley east of the auditorium.

Smith assured us that we should find everything as we wished it when we repaired to the place that evening to witness the spectacular entertainment. He further advised us to make out a program from the great events and scenes of the world. We selected the battles of Waterloo, Bunker's Hill, and Shiloh; Niagara Falls, Yosemite, scenes on the Rhine, the Alhambra by moonlight, and London by gaslight. This programme was forwarded to Smith with the request that he begin at 8 o'clock sharp, and would he please have the man at the crank turn a little slower. Smith, of course, con-

sented. Smith, beyond doubt, was a good fellow; not
a bit like old Bozy — but there, Mr. Bozar was all
right in his way—indeed, a very excellent man in
his way.

On repairing to the auditorium early in the evening, we found a great surprise awaiting us. Instead of
the excavated half-circle with the open sky overhead,
which we thought would be so fine, a vast and magnificent hall received us. The electrical current had not
been applied perpendicularly, but in such a way that a
splendid room had been hollowed out of the solid rock.
Two rows of great gleaming columns, connected later-
ally by massive arches, had been left to support the
high vaulted roof. The shafts of the columns were
highly polished, and dazzlingly white; the capitals were
of new design, but highly artistic and pleasing to the
sight; the base of each column was of a tint wholly
unlike anything we had ever seen, but in exquisite harmony with the pure white of the shafts, and the superb,
though strange tint of the beautiful arabesque work
that carpeted the floor. Between elaborately carved
panels on the walls, and directly opposite to each
other, great spaces had been polished to a brilliancy
far exceeding the best French-plate mirrors. These,
under the powerful but subdued light that came from
a richly chased chandelier pending from the deeply
frescoed ceiling, reflected back, seemingly, for miles and
miles the grandeurs of the apartment. By the right
application of electricity, the electro-magical Smith
could reduce the surrounding stone to dust, or refine
it to the hardness and transparency of crystal, the

solidity of marble, the strength of steel, the lustre of gold. The arch of the opening through which we looked upon the valley beyond was supported by two glistening columns, of crystal purity, so clear that they in nowise interfered with the view. Here, where the eye would oftenest drink in their beauties, the ornamentation and coloring surpassed belief. The electrical tinting had also been applied to the tiers of couches which seated the auditorium. These, though of polished stone, were of such soft hues that we seemed to rest upon down, as we sat or reclined in their luxurious depths. A pleasant warmth suffused the room, and the music of the orchestra came in sweeter cadences by some acoustic principle employed by the electrical architect. It seemed that every sense must be satisfied, and yet we were impatiently awaiting the first act on the programme—anxious for the stirring scenes of war—eager to turn from passive magnificence to witness men contending with shot and shell for a principle, suppressing wrong and tyranny at the point of the bayonet, purchasing homes and liberty with the blood of heroes slain.

It was yet some minutes till 8, and we busied ourselves scanning the marvelous workmanship of the place awed into silence by the splendor of our surroundings. Suddenly a "deep sound strikes like a rising knell!" We looked out, but merely to see the stars twinkling peacefully, far away sentinels of the night. Again we turned to the enjoyment of the warmth and the brilliancy and the music that "rose with voluptuous swell."

> "But, hark! that heavy sound breaks in once more,
> And nearer, clearer, deadlier than before!"

We turned to the opening, and now the famous battle field lay before us, Brussels in the foreground. We looked, just as the cry rang out through the reveling capital—

> "Arm! Arm!" It was the cannon's opening roar."

And then we beheld and heard

> "The mounting in hot haste; the steed,
> The mustering squadron, and the clattering car, that
> Went pouring forward with impetuous speed,
> And swiftly forming in the ranks of war;
> And the deep thunder peal on peal afar."

Apparently ten miles distant from "Belgium's capital," could be seen the smoke of Napoleon's guns opening on the English. Imperceptibly the scene shifted, bringing the plain of Waterloo to the foreground. The battle moved slowly and majestically. We were enabled to see every manœuvre. We could hear the battle cries and death groans. We could see the flash of the combatants' eyes, hear the clinking of the sabers of Milhaud's cuirassiers. There was the man of Marengo, dispatching Generals Domont and Subervic to investigate a body of troops that had appeared in the direction of St. Lambert; there was the "Iron Duke," under the great elm in front of the old mill of Mont Saint Jean, with telescope in hand, watching the movements of his opponents—the one ambitious to conquer the world, the other serving his government, aye, defending English homes. We knew, of course, that

Wellington stood for the right, and rejoiced as the engagement began, that the right was that day to triumph over selfish ambition; but the action was so vivid, true in every detail to the original, the belligerents so real, the two champions so life-like, that we soon felt the personal magnetism of Europe's greatest military genius—the great Napoleon. As the battle approached its crisis, it was not "Blucher or night" that we longed for, but Grouchy with reinforcements for the gallant little corporal. It was with dismay that we beheld on the heights beyond Frichemont the long line of glistening bayonets that told us Blucher was at hand. With consternation we witnessed the repulse of the last heroic charge of the Imperial Guard. With deep sorrow and grief we watched the final rout of the French army as it faded away in the gloom of night, hotly pursued by the relentless Prussians.

Almost regretting that we had elected to see the overthrow of the great military chieftain, we resigned ourselves to the attractions of our royal palace. We were surprised out of our sadness, in part, by the transformation which had been worked in the appearance of the columns. Each one seemed draped with the continental flag, the stars and stripes. Such was the skill of the artist that the flags apparently fell in full flowing folds from capital to base. The thirteen stars of each glowed as if distilled from the patriotic fires that burned in the hearts of the heroes of '76. The intensity and lustre of the red, white and blue spoke of the glory of the incomparable battles fought in the cause of liberty.

Presently the sound of martial music saluted **our** ears. A provincial band, a poor one, consisting **of fife** and drum, was playing Yankee Doodle, and **all** thoughts of Napoleon were carried away by the rising tide of patriotic feelings that swept over us. Boston and vicinity, by starlight, now lay before us. The occasion of the music was the mustering of a body of troops, probably one thousand men, which, as we learned from the orders given, were to proceed to Bunker Hill and form an entrenchment. The gallant Prescott led the detachment past Bunker **Hill** to Breed's Hill. The shadowy forms quickly threw up breastworks. Then followed the rosy flush of dawn in the east; the beams of the rising sun, dancing across the waters of the bay; the surprise of the British at the Americans' bold advance; the cannonade from Copp's Hill, and the ships in Boston harbor; the two attempts to storm the redoubt; the final successful assault, and the retreat of our brave troops across Charlestown Neck to Prospect Hill.

We were again surprised, but not agreeably, on directing our attention to the decorated columns, for while one row was still adorned with the stars and stripes, to which had been added many stars, yet the other row was equally transplendent with the stars and bars. There was none of us but would have preferred to see some mark of inferiority in the emblems of the South. During the battle that was now waged our eyes frequently turned to the flags in hopes of seeing some diminution in the effulgence of the stars and bars. But during the remainder of the evening's en-

tertainment they continued to glow with a lustre equal
to our own flags. It was 2 o'clock in the morning before the program was finished.

On the following day we asked Smith concerning
the flags. He answered: "The first flags I arranged
as I thought would be most pleasing to yourselves,
and so deferred to your patriotism as not to display
the British colors at all. In the latter instance I sym-
bolized the contending parties from our own standpoint. Can you not see that the rebellion was a necessity in the course of progress? Theoretically it is
pleasanter to conceive of progress without the necessity of these bloody eruptions; but here again things
must be taken as they are, and not as they should be.
As rebellions are necessary, so are rebels. The Confederates were fixed forms—forms that must reappear at
every recurring cycle, and through which must flow the
never ending stream of personalities which must
eventually carry your own personalities to those forms
which you are wont to regard with too much bitterness. Contemplating the fact that you must finally
animate those forms, is it not better to recognize the
fact that they fought with a valor and bravery equal
to your own? There needed a fierce heat to forge certain elements of national strength, and shall the car-
bon be deemed less than the oxygen?"

We changed the subject, and hastened to ask for
further particulars in regard to their industrial system.
Mr. Smith gave us many particulars. By subsequent
inquiries made from time to time we gained the full
details of the system, which, I am glad to see, have

been presented in a fascinating work entitled "Looking Backward."

Mr. Lesage, anticipating that great crowds would throng to the mountain to hear and behold these wonderful things, when we should have made them known to the world, announced his intention to apply electricity to the improvement of the roadway that led up to the retreat. There were innumerable hills to be reduced, and as many depressions to be filled up, and the entire road to be widened and leveled. The matter was laid before Smith. He assured us that it would be a great pleasure to himself and his government to assist us gratuitously for a season, but that later, when the value of their assistance should become generally known, and in view of the demands that would be made on them, they would exact payment from the nations of earth for all services rendered. This, it seemed to us, made it useless to expect any national advantages from our discovery, for how could the people, individually or collectively, do anything for the inhabitants of the far away planet? We had been selfishly congratulating ourselves on the fact that while we should reap great benefits from Saturn, it was impossible for us to make any return. Smith explained, saying: "Should we blind ourselves to everything but the present, it would also seem to us impossible for you to make any return. But knowing that we must finally tenant the miserable forms that we see throughout the nations of earth, it is very plain that you can assist us by assisting them. It is humanity that we ask in return for what we shall give. You will ask why we do not help the sufferers directly, as it is in our power to do. But that would be at the expense of your nation's growth in morality and sympathy. Besides, without the nation's help and support, there are among you the strong-handed and keen-witted that would immediately wrest the benefits from those for whom they are intended. True, we might smite these latter; but this again is not in accordance with the best morality."

After the manner of those who have more regard for the present than the future, we deferred the serious consideration of these thoughts to some other time, and warned our obliging genie out on the road. That afternoon Smith was out working the road, and a splendid workman he proved. It would take some time to put the road in good order, and road building became our regular work for a few weeks. Even with Smith's assistance it required a great deal of work on our part in planning, surveying and trudging back and forth. It was a great stimulus to us to see the rapid progress we made. To behold the broad, even road that resulted from our joint exertions, extending itself a full half mile a day, made our labor a pleasure, so that in the evenings we were never too tired to enjoy the novel entertainments that Smith nightly gave us. On going to the auditorium the second evening we found that a great space which had been left in the front portion unseated had been lowered, bringing it much below the level of the lake. A beautiful fountain, a marvelous combination of gold, alabaster and sparkling waters, now flashed back the light of the chandelier. A great pool of clearest water, fed by a miniature cascade, surrounded the fountain. Encircling the pool was a wide border with a rich garniture of grass, delicate flowers, shrubs and a few ornamental trees. That these were all the result of Smith's art in stone-work, made them none the less pleasing to the eye. From such surroundings we studied the great events of history, or drank in the beauties of nature's greatest masterpieces, as presented to our view by the Electro-Camera-Lucida-Motophone.

Thus pleasantly employed, the days went by like hours, and before we knew it the two months' vacation had nearly expired. Absorbed in our work we had given the Pardees hardly a thought all this time. The road was about completed, and everything would be in readiness to receive the public about the time we should start for home. We had yet four days in which to take leave of Mr. Smith, Mr. Lesage, and the Pardees. We had returned from a most enjoyable evening at the auditorium, and were discussing our early departure next morning, when we were "called" from Saturn, and to our consternation the auroraphone clicked: "Mr. Bozar heard from. It appears that he escaped the dummies, and in the unsettled times following the revolt, had accepted a position with a foreign nation. He has lately read an account of our renewed communications and hastened to inform our government that such communications are illegal, and must be immediately suppressed; that the nature of the offense that our nation received from the people of earth will not admit of explanation or pardon; that he had once destroyed your instrument, and that any other that you may have constructed must also be destroyed. Our government, I regret to say, has ordered me to annihilate your 'auroraphone,' and I must obey. I cannot tell you how grieved I am at this, and, just between ourselves, I honestly wish the dummies had done for Bozar while they were at it. Profit by what you have learned, and ever remember me as a friend. JOHN SMITH."

A few moments later there was a terrific crash, and we knew the auroraphone was no more.

CHAPTER X.

A SUBSTANTIAL APPARITION.

WITH the first light of morning we were out inspecting the damage which had been worked by the electric bolt. The auroraphone, auditorium and orchestra had been completely demolished. Never again should we hear the swelling chords of that grand natural orchestra. Never? No, not never. In the course of the cycles we should again listen entranced to the divine music it had so freely discoursed. Yes, and we should again witness the grand scenes which Smith had been reproducing for us. We had also had a glimpse of the wonders of Saturn, a foretaste of what we might expect when in the progress of the soul, or personality, it reached the organisms that people Saturn. We could begin to vaguely realize the complexity and magnificence of the life in the older and grander systems that studded the universe,—life that must eventually be ours also. Existence was a stupendous thing. We were not to pass from time to eternity when this life ended; we were already in eternity to pass in the descending scale of permutation from degradation to degradation, and to pass in the ascending scale from grandeur to grandeur, both of character and physical surroundings.

We returned to the house and made preparations

for immediate departure. It was sad, indeed, to leave Mr. Lesage just after the destruction of his instrument and the blasting of his bright dreams of the pleasure and instruction which the world was to receive through his scientific experiments. He was very cheerful, however, considering everything, and if he regretted the loss of Smith and his electricity more than our departure, he disguised it admirably, and we bid him adieu feeling that the old gentleman was greatly grieved to see us depart.

Thanks to Smith we had a splendid road, and our journey down the mountain was made with more speed and comfort than usual.

A day with the Pardees, and we were ready for the home trip. Rose and Mel, to judge from their cheerful demeanor, had hit upon some compromise, though I half suspected that their high spirits were affected to disguise the sadness of parting. I watched Rose carefully to learn, if possible, whether they had come to an understanding or not. Mel, since I had endeavored to persuade him from his path of duty, as he regarded it, had grown very taciturn, and I could not elicit even a hint from him as to the true state of affairs. It was evident from the extreme sadness of Rose's countenance in unguarded moments that the course of true love was as turbulent in their case as in all others.

The Pardees accompanied us to the station to see us off. Several of our mountaineer friends had also assembled at the station in honor of the occasion. Among these was one whom we had not seen since he rode away after telling us the story of the Lovers'

16

Pool—"Bill Mundy, Esq." He was overjoyed to see us, and we were equally delighted to see him. Mr. Mundy, according to report, had become a model man. He was a law abiding citizen, a member of the school board, and anti-pugilistic to a severe degree, for one of his pugnacious temperament.

Our train was an hour late, and the west bound express came in while we were waiting. Five passengers got off—a gentleman and lady, and three children. The gentleman and lady were at once recognized as Mr. and Mrs. Moses Skein, who, after so many years, had concluded to forget the past, and had come back to surprise Jennie's brother and his wife with a friendly visit. Never dreaming but that Mr. Mundy had learned of their escape from drowning in the pool, nothing had been said to him about Mose and Jennie in the few moments' conversation we had had with him. He had not learned of it, however, and at first he was the picture of fright—terribly scared at what he took to be apparitions. Then as it was hurriedly explained to him that Mose and Jennie had not drowned themselves, the suppressed warlike tendencies that had been accumulating all these years began to flare up. The means employed in his conversion, he hotly concluded, constituted a gigantic fraud. and he proposed to have revenge on the perpetrator forthwith. "The sneaking, white-livered, lying cuss," he furiously exclaimed, "to play ghost on an old friend, and make him believe in speerets and angels, and that he must be awful good, or get everlastingly roasted. By the etarnal, I'll larn him to play ghost on me. I'll maul him for every mother's

son he's cheated me out'er licking for these ten years,"
and despite the many hands put out to detain him, the
sinewy Hercules strode toward Skein with clenched fists
and flashing eyes. Skein, whose muscular proportions
indicated that he was fully capable of defending himself, stood perplexed and half amused at his old friend's
unreasonable rage. Mundy, burning with the desire
to pulverize him, precipitated himself with the fury of
a mad bull against Skein, or rather against his fist,
for Mose had launched that useful member squarely
between Mundy's eyes, and the latter measured his
length on the station platform. He raised himself to
a sitting posture, remarking: "It's powerful sartin
you ain't no ghost now." Several laughed, and
Mundy continued, as he raised to his feet: "This air
a durned funny thing, and no mistake. Guess I ort to
be laughed at, and I begin ter see the fun of it myself.
There's no one as can say that sense can't be pounded
inter Bill Mundy's head, and I reck'n Mose 's got er
fust-class certificate for teaching that way. Shake
hands, Mose, and I agrees right here to stay converted,
ghosts or no ghosts."

Deeply interested in these proceedings, we had hardly
noticed that our train was in. The bell was clanging,
and the conductor's "All aboard!" warned us to
hurry. We had no time for farewells, and with a wave
of our hands from the rear platform of the sleeper we
bid adieu to our mountain friends.

CHAPTER XI.

"HAPPILY EVER AFTER."

My companions accompanied me to my home in Kansas, but finding little to interest them in the city of departed greatness, they pushed on in a few days to their homes in the east.

My health had been wonderfully improved in the mountains, and following my cousin's advice, I settled up my affairs as soon as possible, and at 1:20 A.M., the fashionable hour for departing from the city, I stole out of the place with a grip and a sigh—the total assets of six years' financial operations in the West—a victim, not of Kansas, but of my own cupidity and inexperience. I returned to Colorado Springs. It was at the latter place that I received the following letter from Mel:

———————, KANSAS, Nov. 5, 1889.

Mr. S. I. Karbun,

DEAR COUSIN:—Yours of Oct. 1st at hand. I was glad to learn of your migration to the Springs, and am confident that you will never regret it.

I am at work, and gaining a good practice in my new location. Since you acted so promptly on my advice, I could not do otherwise than act upon yours, though, as you had such a beautiful and eloquent second in Rose Pardee, perhaps I shouldn't give you all the credit. I had concluded that there was no other course but to follow your counsel and begin practice with the intention of taking a vacation next fall to get married. Having fully determined on this, I at once informed Rose by letter of my capitulation. Rose,

244

to my surprise, expressed her willingness to marry me immediately if I still insisted. As I had been insisting so long, I was fearful of again showing any haste. I left it to Rose to name the day, suggesting Christmas as my preference. Rose consented on condition that our wedding trip should be nothing more than a journey to our home here in Kansas, as she couldn't think of my leaving my patients for more than a few days. You must excuse me for dwelling so long on my own affairs, but the occasion is one of a lifetime, and you will make allowances, I am sure.

I suppose you are still a permutationist, as I shall have to call you. I must confess that the more I think of the Industrial Army system, the more fully I am convinced that it affords the only solution of the labor problem. It would be a grand thing, indeed, if the people of the United States could bring themselves to adopt it, and thus lead the world in the grand reform. I must concede that the greatest obstacle is the deep-rooted injustice that has been fostered by the current religion. If our civilization is a Christian civilization, then it can no longer be denied that injustice is an outgrowth, to some extent, of our popular creeds. I very much doubt if a people so influenced by our religion will readily adopt a system so pre-eminently consistent with justice as the Creetan's Industrial System. Hence, I begin to feel the need of a religion of greater justice, and I suppose that in looking about for a more just religion we need not stop short of that religion of complete justice founded on the permutation of personality. Do not think that I am repudiating the faith that has so long been my strength and consolation. It is only when I get to thinking and reasoning deeply on these subjects that I feel any misgivings about the old faith, and, as you know, our religion does not favor the habit of reasoning often or profoundly in an independent way, so it is but seldom that I am troubled with doubts.

Your health permitting, do not fail to be present at my wedding. I shall send you cards later. I trust your health is still improving, and I sincerely hope that you have overcome that foolish whim of dying a celibate. You failed to answer my last letter, but knowing how busy you are in writing up our trip, I have overlooked it this time, but should it occur again, there will, probably, be an affair between us with a monkey-wrench and bit, and considering our skill with those weapons, fatal results to both principals may be predicted. Hoping to hear from you soon,

I remain, yours truly,

MELVIN SIMMONS.

A few days later I received the wedding card, and what was my surprise to read:

Mr. and Mrs. William Harland

request your

presence at the marriage of their daughter

Rose Harland,

to

Melvin Simmons,

Wednesday, December Twenty-fifth,

Two o'clock, P. M.,

1889.

Mr. Harland's farm joined Mr. Simmons', and Rose Harland I had known ever since she was a wee babe. It was the most natural thing in the world that she and Mel should fall in love with each other, and Mel could never have doubted that I knew whom he meant when he spoke of Rose as his affianced wife. He had shared his troubles with Rose Pardee, and she, too, had advised him as I had. "What then," I asked myself, "could have been the cause of Rose's tears and sadness?" Not simply her affection for me, though I was now convinced that Rose had given me her love. No, it was the humiliation of having revealed that love, only to have it received with apparent indifference and disdain.

I lost no time in writing Rose, giving her a full account of my mistake in regard to her and Mel, assuring her that whether I was right or wrong in supposing that she loved me, I was hopelessly in love with her—hopelessly, because I could never bring myself to burden her with the care of an invalid husband. She was young, handsome, wealthy, and some good and worthy man must soon win her love. I could not prove my love for her better than in thus giving her up. I should prove recreant to the religion I professed if I hesitated to do my plain duty, as laid down in that religion, which enforced consideration for the best welfare of others. Consideration for her welfare left me no other course than to protect her from the annoyances that would inevitably attend a matrimonial alliance with one of my irascibility and carping disposition.

Rose answered, frankly confessing that she had loved me, and that no words could tell the humiliation she had experienced for having so boldly intimated it, when she came to realize that I only despised her for it, as my actions seemed to imply. She could easily understand how I had made the mistake, and she appreciated my self-renunciation while I thought she loved another, but she had no sympathy for my present sacrificial spirit. If the world was progressing, as she believed it was, there should come a time when one could be true to his religion without becoming a fanatic. Fanaticism had, beyond doubt, been necessary in the past, at an earlier stage of development, but she hoped and believed that that time was past. She thought that I over-estimated my faults, though she was willing to admit that I did have some. There was no denying that I was over-sensitive, too exacting, and, perhaps, more peevish than I should be. (I began to doubt it for the first time in my life, and as I read over the list the second time I denied it outright.) But if she was willing to assume the responsibility of an invalid husband, she was twenty-two, and ought to know what she was doing. I surely could not doubt the depth of her affection, on the plea of her being a fortune hunter. One of my faults, she thought, was wanting to be coaxed, a peculiarity of children and invalids, and she would again risk a criticism of her womanliness, and humor my whim, by begging me to reconsider the matter, and be reasonable.

I surrendered, and was "reasonable," as Rose counted reasonableness. It was not the grand, heroic thing to do. True, my health had greatly improved, but not to an extent that made my capitulation consistent with the high moral ideal of the religion of permutation. But before judging me harshly, remember that my religion, making celibacy in my case such an imperative duty, had none of that hereditary force that so materially aids the devotee of the older religions. Converts to a faith are prone to think before their conversion, that when they do accept it they will never violate one of its rules or precepts. But once accepted, they soon come to regard it as no indication of their insincerity, that they repeatedly fall in the path of duty, so hard is it to make our lives conform to our ideals. It must not be charged against my religion that I so soon fell short of its requirements. It will take time to get that clear realization of the full import of the permutation of personality to make it a moral power. But the mere thought that we may eventually have to stand in the place of others—that as we do unto others so will we be done by—will go far toward exciting a broader sympathy for humanity. Permutation surely foreshadows the inauguration of a social system of justice and equality, and already its spirit moveth upon the hearts of mankind, and must lead on to complete triumph over selfishness, ignorance and crime. I see it moving on to such a glorious consummation, accelerating its speed at every advance forward; now scintillating broadcast the bright sparks of honesty, justice and sobriety, then in still broader circles radiating the warm beams of faith, of love, of charity; again, it expands into a thousand beautiful virtues of which the ear hath not heard, nor the mind of man conceived; still widening in its sweep, it gathers all mankind into a loving brotherhood, and bears them forward on the broad, bright pinions of the liberty of thought and the knowledge of immortality, till midst the brilliancy of blazing eternal truths, and the mighty thunders of a world's anthem of jubilee, all are enveloped in the glorious halo of the long heralded millennium.

THE END